THE PONZI MAN

DECLAN LYNCH

HACHE
BOO
IRELAND

First published in 2016 by Hachette Books Ireland

A CIP catalogue record for this title is available from the British Library.

ISBN 978 1 47362 769 7

Typeset in Cambria by redrattledesign.com
Printed in Great Britain by Clays Ltd, St Ives plc

Hachette Books Ireland policy is to use papers that are natural, renewable and recyclable products and made from wood grown in sustainable forests. The logging and manufacturing processes are expected to conform to the environmental regulations of the country of origin.

Hachette Books Ireland
8 Castlecourt Centre
Castleknock
Dublin 15, Ireland

A division of Hachette UK Ltd.
Carmelite House
50 Victoria Embankment
London EC47 0DZ

www.hachettebooksireland.ie

For Katie

CHAPTER 1

I like to tell this story because it is true.

The place next to this bar used to be a chip shop, run by an Italian man called Masarella. He had a wife and two sons called Anthony and Paolo, who were about the same age as me, five or six. I don't remember much about the two boys, except that I was playing with them one day on the path along the promenade when a car came up the main street and Anthony ran out in front of it, chasing a ball.

I knew he was going to die. I had a moment of terror, made absolute by the fact that I had kicked the ball he was chasing, too excited by the game to look where he was going. He had run out in front of the car so quickly that it couldn't possibly swerve to avoid him; it was obvious that it was going to hit him.

But it didn't hit him.

I am sitting here now, taking a slow drink of Guinness, in this bar called Cooney's – it is still called Cooney's. And I am still feeling some of the terror after all this time. The car slowed down and moved on, and there was Anthony, still alive. Not only was he not dead, he seemed hardly to have noticed what had happened. He just wanted to get on with the game of ball.

He would not have told his mother or father about it, and neither would the younger brother, Paolo, because I got the impression that his father had this intensity about him, as he worked away shovelling the chips into bags, taking in the money, getting it done. A hard-working, serious man, it seemed, a man who could get very angry.

So he almost certainly never knew how lucky Anthony had been, how lucky he himself had been that he hadn't lost Anthony that day. And not knowing about all that was probably a good thing for him, in a lot of ways.

Because about six months later, when I came back to this place for another summer, Masarella's chipper was gone. I heard my mother and father talking about it, how it turned out that the little Italian had been a bastard for poker. And how, one night on the far side of the town, in some all-night game, he had lost his business.

Again, that feeling of fear comes back to me. Though I was

so young, still I was able to understand that something really terrible had happened. That a man who seemed to have such command over the forces of life had somehow let himself be destroyed by other men, due to some weakness inside him.

I did not know at the time that I would experience that fear for myself, way down the line. Sometimes it is good not to know things.

Because if Mr Masarella had eventually found out what had happened to Anthony that day, as a like-minded individual I can imagine him working it out something like this: yes, he had lost his livelihood in a game of cards. He had put himself and his family through a terrible thing but they were still with him. He had stopped gambling and they had moved to another town, where he started another chip shop, and it was doing well. He had even hardened himself against the desire to gamble, so convinced was he that he had no luck in that area, that the gods despised him.

But if he had learned somehow what had happened to Anthony, or what had not happened to Anthony, he would have realised that, in a certain way, he was actually a very lucky man. That the gods may have abandoned him at the poker table, but they had made up for it in such a beautiful way, with Anthony, that it might be time to look again at these matters of fate and fortune. To have another cut at it.

So I like to think that he never knew about that car missing his son, never knew about maybe the best thing that ever happened to him.

One thing he must have known: when he left the chip shop, they renovated it and extended it and turned it into an amusement arcade.

I worked there one summer. There may be some meaning to this, some deeper connection to be made between this early experience and my later decline, but if that was the case, I would probably have made it before this.

My mother was friendly with the people who ran the amusements, and they gave me a great job handing out change for the slot machines. I was about thirteen but I was so tall that I looked sixteen. I was mannerly too, which made me seem older. And I could get to the job in twenty seconds from the house across the road, a bad old place that we rented from some local woman who was too miserable to live in it herself and lived in a worse place somewhere out the country.

I had this office not much bigger than a telephone booth, with a big sign over the door saying 'CHANGE'. I could lean back in the chair and put my feet up on the shelf, and I could listen all day to the jukebox playing 'The Israelites' by Desmond Dekker and 'Can The Can' by Suzi Quatro and 'I'm Not In Love' by 10CC, and I could watch the people working the one-armed bandits. It gave me a position in life, even a bit of authority.

It gave me a pound note a day, some of which I would put back into the slots, winning and losing. I don't remember much about that part of it – I guess the slot-machine method of gambling is so fucking brainless it doesn't really stay with you. I suppose I was bitter and frustrated and angry when I lost, elated when I got the triple cherries and won; there's not much mystery to it. Tonight as I drink these slow, slow pints of Guinness on this black plastic seat, and any other night, I'm not really interested in exploring the origins of addiction. Because even if there are any, and you can actually name them in individual cases, it doesn't matter to me anymore.

I'm all done, with explanations, with analysis, with judgement. The verdict is in and it is clear. I have lost in life, in every way that is relevant to normal people, and in their eyes, I won't be coming back from there. So I am on my own now.

Still I remember things, even if I have no wish to invest them with any meaning, except to say that in some way, for reasons I don't understand, they have stayed alive in my mind.

There was this big woman from Belfast who would come into the amusements every morning as soon as we opened the big doors, and who would stand there feeding a hundredweight of coins into the machines. Almost all the other people who came to the arcade have faded from my memory, but I can still see her there, remorselessly pumping all the change that I could give her into the slots, barely pausing to enjoy the occasional smash of the machine disgorging a jackpot.

I don't think it was just her physical largeness that engaged me so much, and that has stayed with me. It was the way she went about it all with such calm determination, a kind of certainty that she exuded, the purity of her compulsion, the fact that, win or lose, she would never show any emotion.

I never knew who she was, except that she was one of many Northerners who used to come down to the village for a few weeks during the marching season. They would do a lot of drinking, but she did not drink, or smoke, or dance to the music of the bands in the pubs, or stand drunkenly respectful for the national anthem. She didn't have much interest in being with other people, which itself impressed me, in a way that I didn't understand back then.

Most of the time she wouldn't even come to my door to load up with another few pounds' worth of coins, she would just send some kid down.

Other people were all a bit mixed up; it seemed she had figured out what she wanted to do with her life, and she was doing it. I knew this, because those Northern kids, with their tank tops and their parallels and their Doc Martens, kept coming down to me with another pound note, and another, and another, their hands sticky with the candyfloss she bought for them, demanding 5p and 10p and 50p coins, which they would bring to her to feed the machines. And there must have been some of them who weren't wearing the parallels and the boots, who were as nervous as I was in the presence of their friends, but I don't remember them. I remember only the aggressive ones.

Those kids were hard. One of them was a thalidomide victim, who would just tag along with the others when they came to my window, until the day she came to me on her own, looking for change.

'Two fifties,' she said.

I froze, not knowing what to do with the pound note she had in her hand, which seemed to be just a part of her shoulder.

'Take the fuckin' thing, wee boy,' she said.

I did as I was told, crushed in particular by the 'wee boy' – I figured she was younger than I was.

I replaced the pound note with the two fifties and she brought the money back to the big woman, who had no problem taking it from her and dispatching it.

As to where the big woman got the money in the first place, I have no idea and I don't care. Maybe she only did this for two weeks of the year down south, before returning to her secure post in Belfast in the civil service. But I doubt it. She got that money somehow, and then she would make it her business to gamble it away, in the lowest form of all, the fruit machine.

Drinking my slow Guinness here, I go back there and I see myself, the tall, quiet boy with the good manners giving out the change, and I see her, this doomed woman who did not care what anyone thought of her, and I realise that the boy ended up losing more in one hour, in the depths of one night, than that woman could pump away in a thousand summers.

I go back there, not just because I am physically present in this place, but because I never really saw it properly before. I am seeing a lot more things in all their dimensions, now that my own life has stopped.

It is only getting through to me now, after all this time, that a woman who lived in a bungalow up the lane from this pub must have struggled with the weaker side of her nature and failed as surely as I have done. She seemed glamorous to me at the time: in the mind's eye she is elegant in black, with a daughter called Angela, who was around my age and seemed to do most of the outdoor work, shopping and generally walking around. And though I never spoke to Angela, or she to me, I liked her.

I must have had some intuition that her life was difficult, because I liked her character as well as everything else about her. She seemed stoical, dutiful, making the best of what I sensed was a bad situation. Yes, I knew, at some boyish level, that something was wrong there. I even knew that her mother had male visitors, such as Cyril, who worked in the amusements. I knew that Cyril had problems with drink, that he'd received a terrible kicking in a fight outside a pub.

He rarely spoke to me as he did his work fixing the fruit machines and the jukebox. His silence I took as a mark of intelligence and self-possession. He had this great fistful of keys that he used to open the machines, and I respected him for this, for having skills with machinery that I knew were beyond me. So I didn't really get it into my head until the other day, when I fell to thinking about those times, that Cyril was without doubt in an advanced stage of alcoholism, and that Angela's mother was also addicted to whiskey and fags, and that on the night when I saw them coming out of a pub, supporting one another, like wounded soldiers, they were probably nearing the end of a very hard road.

Maybe it only really became clear to me on my way here tonight. Though I am regarded by a lot of people and by myself as a highly intelligent fellow, I am always being amazed by my own slowness about certain things, how I don't get them until twenty years after they've happened, all the situations I misinterpret, and the actions I misconstrue, the incredible mistakes I have made without any feeling at the time that I was wrong.

Innocence you might call it, if you were being kind, but I had no right to be that innocent. So I am remembering these people, and the lousy hands they were dealt by the gods, and I have not yet had to cast my thoughts more than a few hundred yards away from where I am sitting now.

Across the road in that broken-down old house where we stayed, there was a small room at the top of the stairs that was permanently closed. It wasn't locked, but there was some kind of a dresser blocking the door from the inside, which was a surer way of keeping the likes of me out of it – a child might find a key but he could never get through such a barricade. I know, because I tried. Not because I suspected anything in particular, but because my mother and father never talked about it, which I took as a signal that I should not ask about it.

But a sinister energy attracted me to that room from time to time, and I was curious. I didn't want to go in there, but I didn't not want to go in there either, not entirely. So a few times I gathered up my courage and I tried to push open the door, but it was impossible. It was several years later that I was in a pub at the other end of the village and the barman told me that a man had hanged himself in there. He couldn't tell me who the man was, or what he did, or why he had hanged himself, though I don't think he had any connection with our family, except that we started renting the house for the summer not long after he had killed himself, and we felt it appropriate to ignore everything about him.

I think about him sometimes. I know there was a skylight in that room, with a view of the sea. I wonder did he arrange it so that the last thing he saw was the sea?

And when I think of the various reasons why a man might hang himself back then, naturally I am drawn to my own area of expertise – could he have been a gambler devastated by his losses? Somehow it seems too join-the-dots, that image of the kid living in a house with a room specifically dedicated to denial. And then, of all the weaknesses available to him, he falls to the one which created that denial.

Too obvious, really. Which doesn't mean it isn't true.

My uncle Christy, who was some kind of half-qualified accountant or book-keeper and who stayed with us sometimes, went for a slower form of self-destruction, dying of drink-related diseases in the county hospital. He used to buy me 99s in a big shop at the other end of the village selling seaside stuff, beach balls and swimming hoops, and on these days he seemed like a sweet-natured man, though I realise now it was the naggins of whiskey that were getting him through it, helping him to endure the torment of trying to entertain a child. He was always wearing a suit.

And before I was born, my own father took the wrong turn, and never really found his way back. He married the wrong woman and, eventually, he told me about it. He told me that he loved this other woman before he met my mother, and that he broke it off with her by mistake. He had gone to work in Dublin for a while, driving a bus, and he'd heard that she was seen out walking with some other fellow back in the midlands. So he wrote her this letter, ending their relationship.

Turned out that his information was wrong.

He told me this when he was about seventy. We were drinking in the afternoon in this pub near the city centre where we would meet every few weeks. He would come up from the midlands on the bus and we would drink pints for a few hours and then he would get the bus back home. I could have afforded to get him a taxi at that time, I really wanted him to get a taxi, but he preferred the bus. He had been a busman, driving for CIÉ and then for a local bus company. I watched him going off that evening and I wondered what levels of Hell he had endured over the years, regretting his appalling mistake. But I was too engrossed in my own life at the time, really, to empathise.

Maybe he had wanted us to have a long conversation about it, but it seemed more that he wanted to place it on the record, just to share it. Just in case I found out later on, by mistake.

He didn't say that the rest of his life had been diminished by it, though it must have been. He would never question the way that my own life had gone, or offer any advice, probably because he felt he was no great authority on the subject of life. And, anyway, I didn't give the impression of a man who was in any need of advice, of a kindly, steadying father's voice. I was a big shot, after all.

On the days when we would meet I would never feel any great unhappiness coming from him, though I see now that he probably just kept quiet about his fate, the way people did. He was not an obviously tragic individual. He had no addictions, though he did take me to race meetings, which turned out in the end to be unfortunate.

I found this old race card the other day, from the Phoenix Park. We went there a few times. As I turned the pages of the race card I was astounded at how much of it I remembered, the names of the horses, how the races had finished. I thought about the way my father would give me back whatever money I had lost on the horses, in the car on the journey home, and I wondered if that had been wise.

Coming back from Fairyhouse races one evening, in a pub full of punters reflecting on their day's sport, he introduced me to my first bookmaker, one from our town called Walter Jackson. He seemed such an impressive old man to me, with his fine black overcoat and his three-piece pin-striped suit, the same Walter Jackson I had seen earlier at the track standing on a box with a white satchel full of money and emblazoned with his name – ah, those satchels used to make me long for some vaguely imagined future when I would be free, with my hands on great quantities of pound notes.

I remember, too, there must have been a big Gaelic match around that time, because Walter and my father were talking about various large bets that Walter had won on it, just private bets with friends. Walter said he'd been collecting cheques all week on the back of it, and when I asked some childish question about cheques, he took a few from the inside pocket of his overcoat to show me how it worked. My father went to the bar to get a round of drinks, while old Walter, with much earnestness, showed me a cheque for two hundred pounds only, a cheque for five hundred pounds only, a cheque for three hundred and fifty pounds only, which imparted to me an understanding of cheques, but also a deeper understanding that this was how men should live.

Maybe there is something too – not much, but something – in the recollection that not only did my father introduce me to my first bookmaker, he had already introduced me to card-playing, setting up games of pontoon, playing with matches and then with money. 'Let's make this a bit more interesting,' he would say, when we started with the money.

Whatever happened to me, I don't think I could ever blame it on my father. We got on tremendously well. And yet maybe I picked up some weakness from him, not in his liking for the horses and a game of cards, but something that started on the day he wrote the letter to that woman, some strain of misfortune that dictated that grievous error of his, and that somehow passed into my blood.

I never thought enough about this, I never wanted to think about it, because it seemed to bring a story of great sadness too close to my own small tale. I just found it hard to see myself in that broader scene of a man destroying his own happiness in an uncharacteristically careless episode.

But I was right in there anyway.

So it's like all these catastrophes were happening around me, and I kept looking straight ahead, just thinking about the next thing. And when catastrophe came to me at last, I had no way of recognising it. That's what I mean by innocence, I suppose, innocence bordering on unconsciousness. For a long time I never put it all together, not until I came back here.

I'd have another slow pint of Guinness now, my fourth, if I could afford it. But I actually haven't got enough money in my pocket for another and, anyway, three is the perfect number for pints. It took me so long to understand that, another of those things that I did not understand for such a very long time. I would have the three but I could never leave it at that. I would forge on until I was drinking alcoholically most nights. Yet I found my way out of that particular hole, probably because the drink was never what is called my primary addiction. Especially when it started to interfere with the gambling, which for me was always the big show.

I am alone now in the bar on this Friday night in October. The barman is busy in the lounge where the respectable and the ambitious people of the village have always gone, leaving the plain bar to the likes of me and Bobby White.

Christ, I have become linked in my own mind with Bobby White, this poor dirty old fisherman who rarely caught any fish but would come here on dole day and sit on a high stool in the corner drinking bottles of stout. Nothing very bad ever happened to Bobby, except that he lived alone in poverty and squalor. He hardly had what you might call a life for it to be ruined. So any time I came in here as a child, delivering some message, the vibe I got from Bobby was one of contentment, even a modest sort of merriment. He would be chatting to the woman who owned the place as I hurried through. I suppose Bobby's daytime drinking made him seem like a shift worker, except he hadn't done the shift. His true position in life was not to work, but to sit on that high stool drinking bottles of stout. I can see him so clearly there, in his heavy black clothes; I can remember the smell of the stout that was so forbidding to me.

But I did not look down on Bobby. I did not look down on anyone with a low station in life. I was always looking up, to those who had more than I did, to friends who lived in houses that were not horrible, that were not embarrassing.

The woman who rented the house to us could never be

persuaded that the place needed a bit of improvement, that everything in it felt about eighty years behind what it should be, that I couldn't bring anyone into the house for fear that they might see this place from the Middle Ages, these people who lived in proper houses, which seemed beautiful to me.

My mother and father didn't seem to understand that this made me feel inferior to all the middle-class people I knew, and as for themselves, they didn't really care. They just said they were doing this mainly for me, because I had all these friends up here, and I understand now that even if the owner had been normal, and had told them they could fix up the place themselves, they probably didn't have the money.

I probably even understood that back then, renting this place as it was, cheap though it must have been, could be regarded as an extravagance for a busman – they also rented the television, into which I would stare all day at the treasures of the BBC and ITV, which I did not have at home, noting that even the poor characters in English sitcoms seemed to be living in nicer places than this, confirming to me that I had been born into this lower class. That there were certain things to which I was not entitled, and that this was ordained by Nature, no matter how much money I would eventually make, and how much I would lose.

And even now I would say that one of the reasons I am going down, when a lot of others should be going down with me, is that I was not connected to the right people – or, at least, I was not connected to them for long enough.

I count the coins in my pocket, and I reckon I have less money now, in this world, than Bobby White had with which to have a drink, and to have a bet. Yes, after everything, I am still betting.

There will be no redemption for me, just a true acceptance of what I am. Acceptance, at least, by myself.

And I'm only living like Bobby White in certain ways.

Funny thing, but when I worked in the amusements, I would be sent out the back to the mobile home in which Cyril lived, to get him to come in and fix a machine. I thought that that mobile home was beautiful, as beautiful as every other home that was not my own. I would open the door and Cyril would be sitting there in deep silence, watching one of the daytime programmes, *Crown Court* or *Emmerdale Farm* or some black-and-white movie like *Whisky Galore!*, and it would seem wrong to drag him away from this lovely situation to the racket of the machines.

The amusements have now been replaced by a tourist information centre. I am living now, at the other side of the village, in a mobile home.

I will step out into the night, then, and walk along the promenade.

In my mind it is not October, it is July, always July, and it is still bright. It is not quiet: it is busy with young people hanging around in groups, with grinning boys queuing for chips at the window of McCoubrey's café here on the main street, and girls with their hair still wet coming out of the swimming pool carrying their rolled-up towels, everyone somehow knowing their place in the summer evening parade.

I had my place, too, looking at them all through the bars on the side window of our place. Which is not as bleak as it sounds. The bars were needed not for burglars but because the house stood on its own on that side of the street, next to the car park, and when there was a really big crowd in the village on a Sunday, people would lean against the walls and the windows. Some barrier was needed, I guess, to stop them turning their attention to our place, when they were drunk.

There was nothing to keep out the noise of the Northerners talking and arsing around, having their burgers and chips and their cans of Harp on those hot days when the tar was melting on the road, having their few hours of release until it was time to get on board the Ulsterbus again, and go back across the border to the riots and the car bombs. I can still hear them now, cracking away as I sat in our place with the curtains drawn on a sunny Sunday afternoon, watching *The Big Match* or *The Golden Shot*.

I can hear the music from the amusements above it all, on those big days when the jukebox would be connected to a loudspeaker and the records could be heard all over the village. They were slow to get new records in, so I knew every song on that jukebox because I heard them all the time, and I knew most of the numbers assigned to them – A1 was 'Rocket Man' by Elton John, A2 was 'That's The Way

(I Like It)' by KC and the Sunshine Band, A3 was 'Everything I Own' by Ken Boothe, A4 was 'Get It On' by T. Rex – but the one that is always in my head is 'Young Girl' by Gary Puckett & The Union Gap.

Which isn't some illusion on my part. It's not as if my memory has selected that sound as the only one, blocking out the many other records that blared out of the amusements. That song really was in the air much more than any other, in that place, in that time. The obvious explanation is that somebody was crazy about that song, and they kept playing it for years after it had originally been released, but it seemed to go beyond that: it seemed that after several summers the song had become a natural part of the atmosphere, that it was meant to be blasted out into the open air just like this. Again, I'm pretty slow, so it took me a long time to grasp that 'Young Girl' is about a guy feeling down because he's discovered that his lover is below the age of consent. But I really don't think anyone paid much heed to that, even if they got it. You couldn't break it down into individual parts, and you still can't take it back.

I am walking along this promenade a thousand years later, on a dead autumn night, and still I can hear Gary Puckett & The Union Gap caught in that great moment of crisis, pouring it all out. I am not hearing something that no longer exists, fooling myself, escaping into the past the way the Northerners used to escape down here. I feel that I am not wrong: it is the quietness tonight, the deadness, that is wrong.

That music is actually more alive to me now than it was then, because it has stayed in the air somehow, touching my soul. I am not depending on someone else to put it on, it comes on automatically.

These memories appear to me like the offerings on some advertising channel, presenting images to me that I can see, and hear, and which connect me to powerful feelings. But it is not some outside agency that is choosing these images, it is some force inside me, bringing all these things to my mind, not in the exact way that they happened but as something stronger, as clues to a higher understanding. They speak to me of my abandonment, of being excluded from a remembered paradise. And they remind me, too, that that is the fate of everyone.

It is breaking my heart, that song, but I am devouring it, gorging on the music of my youth, and all that it promised. Yes, I believe that everybody does this, that this is just another of the things I didn't understand when I should have done. When finally we grasp the full dimensions of our experiences, we just throw away that moment of supreme enlightenment in this lamenting for our lost years. We don't realise that when we were fifteen we were already lost, that things were no better for us in the past, because even when we were kids we were chasing some remembered paradise. By some illusion it always seemed ahead of us then, at the next party, in the next bottle or the first blast of a cigarette, but deep down we must have known it was already gone.

So there is only the present moment, informed by whatever has happened to us in other such moments. I am hearing 'Young Girl' in my head now, tonight, not on some night a thousand years ago.

I am starting to sing it, as I walk along this deserted promenade. I am not afraid to sing it: I am giving it full voice. There's a sense of drama in the song that suits a good, loud rendition. In an earlier part of my life, I would have been embarrassed to do this; now I remember hearing men singing on this street as they walked past my old bedroom in the early hours, men drunk enough not to care what anyone thought of them. I am not drunk but I am still singing.

I am passing another pub about halfway up the main street, a place that used to be run by a guy called Gerry, who had left his wife and children to have an affair with a woman called Louise, who, in turn, had left her husband and children.

I was in my early twenties and just visiting the village for a few days, when I called in to this pub on a winter's night, to find that there were candles on all the tables. The electricity had been cut off: they couldn't pay the bills because nobody came to the pub anymore. They had transgressed, and they had been ostracised.

I went up to the bar and ordered a pint of Guinness from Gerry, a man I didn't know. He was older than me, about the same age then as I am now. He said he could only give me a bottle because the pumps didn't work. I took the bottle and sat there in the candlelight, in front of the fire. They had lit a fire.

And then Louise came down to sit at the bar. She had a gin and tonic. They talked, just about ordinary things, it seemed, no dramatics. They were grown-up, middle-aged people, who had made this enormous decision, which had turned them into outsiders. Yet they did not move to another town. They did not close the door and hide. I felt there was something heroic about that.

I do not know what happened to them. I do not know if they were happy that they had made the right decision, regardless of the difficulties, or miserable for the rest of their lives. I do not know if one or other of them had been abused in their marriage or if they had been abusers or what. I do not know if they had found a wonderful sense of peace with each other, or if they were just a couple of alcoholics hanging on to one another, going to the bad. Or a bit of all of these things mixed together.

I just saw them that night, sitting in the candlelight, talking quietly. Like my father, each of them had married the wrong person but, unlike him, they had given themselves another shot at it. If you've got about a hundred years to spare, you can add it all up and tell me who came out ahead there.

No, I am not drunk but I am still singing. Maybe some kid is lying in bed listening to me now, making noise on the street and what does it matter? I am just some galoot, and soon I will be gone.

CHAPTER 2

A mobile home feels right for the man who is going down. I am not talking about one of those grand mobile homes that rich Irish people used to maintain in the years when I moved among them, but the sort that I am living in now. An old caravan, really, that has been on this site at the top of the village for a long time, a thing we bought when it was already old, to keep up some sentimental attachment to this place.

It was never meant to be anyone's primary residence, but it's mine now. It's an odd thing but since I moved back here, and set myself up in this caboose, I have started to remember stories of other men who somehow put themselves beyond the embrace of normal society and ended up living in a mobile home, stories to which I did not give much attention at the time – but I am thinking of them now. I can think of at least three of these men who were quite well known: a revered traditional musician, a campaigner for the legalisation of cannabis, a brilliant writer from Galway who went mad, men who probably didn't care much for respectable ways of living in the first place. Or just big-time con artists like me, waiting to be put into jail.

There is something about the impermanence of it that suits us. We don't have much to plan for; we have tried to live like normal people and it went all wrong, so we just want to be left alone now, supping cheap cans of lager and looking deep into the blue flame of the Super Ser.

It was a Super Ser that heated the television room in the old place, too, so I have only to flip that black switch on the gas cylinder and I am thirteen again, thirteen now, thirteen for all time, except I don't have to go back to school in September.

But I have homework to do, of a kind. And I'm trying to avoid getting started on it this morning, though my solicitor will be here soon and he will be expecting something from me.

He wants me to start writing things down. He says that a confession written in a suitable tone of remorse might influence the judge. He wants me to see a counsellor. He says that that would look good, too, when it comes to sentencing. He wants me to go to meetings of Gamblers Anonymous.

He is coming here even though it's a Saturday, because he feels that what needs to be done probably cannot be accomplished within office hours. His name is James Hamilton, and I think he may be a good man.

I have not been helping him. I am not bothering to do any of the stuff he's asking me to do; I am not taking his good advice; I am being short with him.

It is a fault of mine, being short with people who are doing some service for me. I have even lost friends due to my attitude to waiters and barmen, but I don't seem to be able to do anything about it. I don't like it in myself, but it just comes out of me, this need to insist to a waiter in a pretty unpleasant tone of voice that, for example, I really don't want coleslaw, that it's not all right for them just to give me coleslaw anyway because 'If you don't want it you don't have to eat it.' I don't want coleslaw so don't give it to me.

And while this is going on, I can feel that the person I am eating with is hating it, and I am actually hating it myself, this ugliness that comes out of me, like some ancient voice declaring that there will always be some part of me that is an incurable asshole. That even my much better habit of leaving a big tip will not reverse the damage. And it is all the more galling because in almost every situation other than the one of people bringing me food and drink, stretching right back to that first job I had in the amusements, probably back to the day I was born, I have the most excellent manners. I've even read it in the papers, how my manners were one of the main reasons I was able to 'hook people into my schemes', that I always 'looked the part', with my tailored suits and my general attention to the outer signs of affluence. Yes, they were right about the clothes and the grooming, the writing of thank-you notes, the sending of wine to other people's tables. They just missed the bit about me giving waiters a hard time – given how they despise me already, I figure that this is one of the few things I've gotten away with.

But I fear it is another of those things that I am slow to understand, another of the weaknesses I am trying to rationalise, without quite knowing how to just cut it out. I believe that it's based on my own most ancient feelings of inferiority, on the fact that I belong to that class of people who are supposed to do all the waiting for eight euro an hour and be happy about it, that I hate anyone being subservient – so my attitude is a kind of misdirected anger. My lavish tipping would tend to support this fine theory, even to give it some dignity, yet I've got to concede that it usually comes out the wrong way. It usually looks bad in practice because, to put it as simply as I can, there is something wrong with me.

Maybe it's because he's young, or because I'm getting him for free, on the legal aid scheme, that I have shown James Hamilton disrespect. Or maybe it's just the knowledge that I don't have much time left out here in the world, so I resent sharing any of it with solicitors, or counsellors, or with other assholes like myself in damp old halls.

The things that I am feeling now, the things that made me sing on the street last night, are not things I can explain to other people, even if I wanted to.

Still, he comes up here, always wearing a suit. He reminds me of myself in that respect, as does his generally courteous manner. He calls me Mister Devlin. I've been calling him Mister Hamilton back, in a less respectful tone, as if I don't want to get to know him any better.

I'll probably try very hard to be nicer to him today, because I'm still elated after last night in the village, by the few drinks and the ideas it put into my head. Some of which may be the half-formed visions of a wastrel, some of which may be beautiful and true. None of which are admissible in court, which I feel may also be the cause of some of my poor behaviour towards young Hamilton.

I am in a world of cruel legalities now, where the finer thoughts I might have about the issues are of no concern to anyone. If they wanted truly to know my state of mind, I could write down the stuff that was racing through my head last night, but they're not looking for that. These guys don't care about the sound of Gary Puckett & The Union Gap on a summer night a long time ago; they don't know that they, too, are lost; they just want me in and out of their bullshit system in the way that is most agreeable to them.

And I have made it possible for them to do that to me, so I hate myself for it, but still . . .

I can see James Hamilton coming up the lane now. He

reminds me a bit in looks of Neil Mellor, who played for Liverpool, which is useful in one way – he is tall and fair-haired, and he looks strong, like an athlete, even. Which gives me a certain confidence, based on some vague notion that the man defending me might look impressive in a courtroom. Then again Neil Mellor, though he scored the odd important goal and was a real trier, was not quite top class.

'Good morning, Mister Devlin,' he says, and we shake hands. Again I like the way he says it, straight, without a note of condescension, not the 'Mister Devlin' I've heard from some lawyers, with a slight emphasis on the 'Mister' as if there's something inherently amusing about a man in my situation being elevated to the rank of 'Mister'.

'Mister Hamilton,' I say, trying for once to make it sound as if I regard him as an equal. Which I might do, if we'd happened to meet in better circumstances. But the way things are, he's just this guy whose function it is to keep asking me to do things that I don't want to do.

I go to the little kitchen area to boil the kettle for the two cups of tea we usually have, made from one teabag. Today, unlike other days, I will give him the fresh bag, using the sodden one for myself. I'm trying. Jesus, I'm trying.

'I can write that confession for you,' I say, as he opens his briefcase on the kitchen counter and takes out his papers and his laptop, immediately darkening my mood. In the time it takes him to organise the documents I keep talking.

'I can write the confession, I can go to Gamblers Anonymous . . . I just don't want to,' I say.

He smiles, taking his mug of tea. I've given him the one that is clean and white inside. 'You will do nothing . . . at all?'

'I don't have the time, Mr Hamilton . . . just do not have the time,' I say.

Which comes out sounding funnier than I meant it to be. We both laugh.

I'm sitting across the narrow little counter from him now, on the soft corner seat. Both of our laptops are open, facing one another. With the curved table and the curved seating, it feels like we're in some sort of a cheap café.

'You might find that it helps to write it down, to share all this in some way. Helps you personally, not just in terms of your sentence,' he says.

'They already know every bet that I had, every race I punted on, every game of football, every winner and every loser. It was all online.'

'But your dealings with your clients. The sense of . . . remorse you feel about losing their money in that way. Some of them were close personal friends.'

'Remorse? What good is that to them?'

He drinks his tea – an act of courtesy in itself in the circumstances – and thinks about it. 'It might be good for you,' he says.

'But I do feel remorse. I feel it all the time. I feel like a complete asshole . . . which is what I am.'

He considers this. 'I know a guy who stole from the bank he worked in. About half a million. Same as yourself, online gambling. Threw himself into the fellowship of Gamblers Anonymous, got a year suspended from the two years he got, and was in an open prison within six months. From what I can make out, this is how the system works now.'

It sounds so reasonable, what he says, and I can see it working for other people. It's just that what works for other people doesn't work for me these days. 'The way you put it, if I do all that you say, the system will end up owing me some time,' I say.

'You have to give yourself every chance.'

'But I'm different. I mean, you know I'm different.'

He knows I'm right but he recovers. 'Judges aren't supposed to take the notoriety of the defendant into account. They're above reading the papers.'

'It was millions . . .'

'Whatever sentence you get, with the right attitude you can get some taken off it.' He seems sincere, this Hamilton. He seems to be trying his best, more than is strictly necessary. On a Saturday too.

Still, I am holding my ground. 'I'll tell you about my attitude . . . I'm still gambling,' I say. I gesture to my laptop, which is open on a betting website. I'm getting the internet from the house next door, which was a delightful discovery, another little display of kindness to me from the baleful gods. This morning I have already won 140 euro on tennis matches in some low-class tournament in France.

He seems defeated by this for a moment, but he keeps going. 'As I understand it, Gamblers Anonymous only requires you to have a desire to stop gambling. Nothing else, just a desire to stop gambling,' he says.

'Well . . . I don't even have that,' I say.

'Even after everything?'

'I don't see it as gambling anymore, not really. In fact not at all. Betting is my only possible source of income now. I'm actually living off it. I'm not living very well, as you can see, but I am living. I can even afford the odd pint of Guinness.'

'Even after everything . . . I don't know how you can still be at it,' he says, not in a judging tone but with a sense of mystery.

'I'm actually a good gambler. Most gamblers are bad gamblers. I'm good,' I say.

Hamilton leans forward, genuinely engaged. 'But you lost so much?'

'It's the sort of thing you can't explain to them in a courtroom. It's very strange, very subtle.'

'How it gets away from people?'

'Smart people.'

'So you're smart . . . and still you won't help yourself by jumping through a few of these hoops?'

'I've got all this other stuff going on in my head,' I say.

He goes quiet for a few moments. 'I've been told to mention the singing to you,' he says, as if reluctant to intrude on my private issues.

For a moment I am surprised. Then I am just surprised that I'm surprised. I might get away with being rude to waiters and with a bit of internet access but I'm not getting away with anything else.

'The singing . . .' I say.

'I had to call in to the sergeant about something else and he said that he'd had a few complaints about you singing on the street late last night.'

'You see? I haven't a fucking hope.'

And maybe that is part of the reason for my reluctance to engage with the conventional forces of rehabilitation and recovery. Maybe if you're going to do all that, you need to have a hope. You need something waiting at the end of it. A job you like. Maybe some children. A woman.

All I have is a mobile home and a wife somewhere up in Dublin who despises me, and this strange feeling that I am on the brink of discovering the meaning of life.

Hamilton looks away. He seems to be struggling with something. Then he manages to get it out. 'You knew my father,' he says.

I think little of it. Running quickly through the lads I used to know around here, I can't recall a Hamilton.

'Edward Brennan,' he says.

'Ed,' I correct him.

Ed Brennan . . . knew him very well. I knew him during the summers I spent here. He played in a band and I was the manager, which really meant that I just hung around with them, trying to meet girls. Calling in to the owners of halls and lounge bars to ask for a gig, a time during which I started to develop some of the fine manners that took me so far in life.

I was always in Ed's big house way over on the other side of the village from where we are now. Ed's people were rich.

'Edward . . . Ed is my father,' he says, still sounding slightly embarrassed to be letting this personal detail intrude on our professional relationship. 'My biological father,' he adds, in case I missed that embarrassment.

'I knew Ed,' I say.

'I have my mother's name . . . Stella Hamilton,' he says.

Stella Hamilton was known to me, too. And I can see something of Stella in him, his blondness, a certain air of earnestness, of optimism. But I can't see much of Ed yet, because Ed was dark but mainly he was big, very big, on the cusp of being fat. James Hamilton is big, but not in that way.

Ed was big, but he was also strangely light on his feet. I can still see the way he used to move through one of the pubs his father owned, emptying ashtrays and straightening chairs with that peculiar grace of movement, a concentrated energy, getting everything ready before it opened.

Then James Hamilton tells me about it. How Ed has gone to the bad. Drink, in Ed's case, maybe a bit of the gambling, too, but mainly the drink. And though I was riffing last night about catastrophe being an everyday thing, there's something that rattles me about the catastrophe of Ed Brennan.

His son is here telling me that Ed still lives in the big house, but he's on his own now. He has fathered four children, with three different mothers – one of them Stella Hamilton – and though Ed seems to have plenty of money, the children were looked after in ways that didn't rely on Ed for their administration. Ed had become an irredeemable asshole, even to his own mother and father, whom I remember as nice people, or about as nice as rich people can be.

The man telling me this without anger or disdain is a beneficiary of their wisdom. They paid his way through college and arranged for him to be set up with an established law firm. He says he hasn't spoken to his father for about two years, not because he doesn't want to but because Ed has shut himself away drinking and will speak only to other drunks and degenerates. I guess that James sees me as belonging broadly in this class of down-going men, that something in my demeanour has reminded him of them.

He pauses, then takes out his phone and finds a text he received that morning, the first communication of any kind he had had from his father for a long time. 'He'd like to meet you,' he says.

How strange it is to hear those words, to be told that some other human being wants to meet me, would like to meet me, someone to whom I have done no wrong – or none that I can recall. 'That's nice,' I say.

James lets a snort out of him, like he can't help it when he hears the word 'nice' in relation to Ed. In relation to the two of us. 'I would advise very strongly against it,' he says, with all his earnestness.

'You mean . . . when everything is going so well?'

James studies his phone, ignoring my defeatism. 'I'll say this . . . he must have a lot of time for you . . . sending a text when he could just come and knock on the door . . . it's like he actually appreciates you may have other things to deal with right now.'

'Right . . . and that wouldn't be like him?'

James shuts off the phone, still trying to figure the meaning of this. 'To kind of ask permission, that really is something,' he says.

'Maybe he's asking your permission too,' I say.

James doesn't answer. He just looks at me with an air of bafflement, as if I've said something ridiculous.

I guess old Ed really burned a few bridges there along the way.

CHAPTER 3

So James Hamilton, the son of Ed Brennan, sent here to help me, is complicating my life a little further. Not that he wanted to, but he passed it on anyway, that Ed would like to see me. Like it's his duty, as a professional.

Marvellous, really, how detached he seems from his own father, how he's reporting this to me as if Ed is just another of his asshole clients, maybe a special one but still just . . . some guy.

A lot of bridges there, maybe some still burning.

James is saying he could take me for a drive past the house, which is still a fine big modern house but the immaculate front lawn and the garden, which everyone remembers, are now growing wild, and have been since the day Ed's mother passed away, four years ago. He says it all looks drab and dirty now, the home of a beaten man. And there's a body of opinion that Ed, from time to time, is making his money by running some kind of an all-night bar and a bordello in there. That he is Tony Soprano not just in his physical presence but in the way he has rejected everything that is decent and responsible.

Straight away I figure it crudely like this – in his youth Ed had been given too much, he had been too happy. After that, everything must have seemed a disappointment. I can see it clearly now, this vision of the house in its state of dissipation, which James is describing to me, but I'm seeing it just as clearly the way I knew it, remembering certain scenes that have stayed with me, in the peculiar way that these things do. One such scene has Ed playing the drums along with a Led Zeppelin record, this crazy noise in the room – the stereo was fabulous, with a quality of sound so superior to any other I have ever heard; it must have been some limited edition, for specialist use, not for the general public. And there was Ed pounding the drums with all his strength, his feet working the bass pedal and the hi-hat, slamming down on the snare drum to match the screaming guitar of Jimmy Page. I had never heard such loudness.

I see him, too, playing those drums quietly along with 'Bell Bottom Blues' by Derek and the Dominos, a song that means more to me today than it did then, now that I've got these blues of my own.

I see the Ed of today sitting down there in that same room, the drums long gone, listening to Hank Williams as he drinks. We love Hank Williams, all of us down-going men. We know that Hank knows the state we're in. His voice, with its desperate loneliness and its powerful sadness, is our voice.

So, I don't want to think about the Ed of today. I still want to think of him in the summer of that beautiful time, with the girls gathered around him at some party in his house. I remember one of them saying to me that Ed was not the best-looking but he had this magnetism. He was completely at ease with his own largeness, to the extent that I wonder if he registered it at all, if he just felt that everyone else was undersized. And I think he understood that thing about giving women your complete attention. Or maybe they just liked being with a guy who had so much going for him.

I don't know, I was just a spectator in that game. Slow in this, too, I had no idea how to make anything happen with females until most of my youth was gone. I saw everything about myself as wrong: being tall was wrong, having red hair was wrong – even though it is actually strawberry blond, which is much better than red – all the shit I used to talk about music was wrong and, of course, being the son of a busman was wrong. I would look at Ed there, so integrated into all that great stuff from which I seemed to be excluded, and I knew that his life was much better than mine.

But he brought me in there, and I loved him for that. He asked me to be the manager of this teenage band in which he played the drums, in which he was the most talented by a long way. He brought me to his father's pub in the town where Ed would hire bands playing good music at ridiculous volume. I saw a band one night opening up with the hard-driving blues of 'Pledging My Time' by Bob Dylan. I was sitting right at the front and the sound of the harmonica pierced so deeply into my skull I think it is still in there somewhere. I even remember acutely the taste of the dark red ale I was drinking, back when I was just starting on the ale.

So maybe Ed had been given too much, had been too happy. Eventually he had taken over the running of his father's pubs and he had probably done all right at that, but in his heart he had wanted to be a musician, a drummer with a proper rock band. And he was a really fine, solid drummer but it never happened for him, not because he didn't have it but because of something else I have found to be true – it doesn't happen for most people. He got no further than that teenage band, and they were no worse than most teenage bands, I guess, and sometimes in the world such a band makes it, and sells ten million records. It just wasn't going to be them. But they were decent lads who accepted me as the manager, even though I was a stranger who had no idea what I was doing, and there wasn't much to manage, bullshitting with Ed about being massively successful, helping them to hump the gear into village halls.

Ed could see that one going down easily enough, because he knew his music, and that was how I knew him – we went to the same record shop in the town, where we bought the same kind of records, the superior kind, which gave us a sense of brotherhood. But the music did not free our spirits completely without the bottles of Harp lager that we also favoured, and the naggins of vodka, going down easier all the time. And we got away with it too, thriving on it, really, roaming wild on it, apart from an odd phase when I was eighteen when I thought a lot about hanging myself, like the guy in the room at the top of the stairs. I knew I wasn't going to do it, I just thought about it, assuming at the time that everyone else was thinking about such things after a few drinks.

Eventually I was able to cut down on the drinking, like I said, to devote my energies to the money game. But Ed has cut down on nothing, they say. He's still out there, doing whatever he does, whatever he likes.

Maybe we are dead most of the time, guys like me and Ed. It is only the adrenalin of a bet or a drink that gets us going, loving the game because we are not loving anything outside the game. And when even that goes bad on us, we end up in these places, in this mobile home of mine or in the house in which Ed spends his days, Ed who has sent this message that he would like to see me.

'I'll have to think about it,' I say to James.

I quite enjoyed saying that, involving as it does the exercise of some personal choice on my part, even the idea that I might be doing someone a favour.

'I should tell him to stay away, really. Will I just do that?'

'Nah, I can handle it.'

James Hamilton winces. He stares at his phone for a bit, trying to work it out. 'As a solicitor, I have to say again that I would not encourage you to spend time with my father,' he says.

'As a solicitor . . . and as a human being?'

'As a human being I feel the same way.'

We have a decent laugh at this, but we know that Ed has somehow inserted himself again into both of our lives, and that it may be difficult to get him out. Even ignoring him has its complications: it might offend him.

James sends the text, which says simply, *OK*.

I have a sense of that message leaving his phone and travelling all the way from here back to my youth. They're all gone now, all those people who went to Ed's house. A lot of them were from the town, and are either still living there, or in Dublin, or London, or Toronto. At least two are dead. The only ones I know of who can still be found in this village where we were all young together are Ed and now me. Even with all the fun gone out of it, even with the amusements gone, even with that tourist information centre where the amusements used to be, it is still a beautiful place. But I don't care about that anymore and neither, I imagine, does Ed.

CHAPTER 4

All I've got now is this inner life. The only place they can't get me now is inside my head. The only time they can't take away from me is the past.

But this afternoon I feel like making an effort anyway, to give James Hamilton some of the bullshit he's looking for. Some version of what these guys regard as the facts, but which have little truth in them, little of the complexity of real experience.

In this bogus version I am the bad guy at every point of the journey, and I acknowledge my badness. Even though sometimes I don't believe I'm much worse than most men and, as I said to James, I don't even think I'm a bad gambler.

I've won another ninety euro since he left, on the Saturday racing at Newbury.

I saw him walking away after our talk this morning, stepping around the puddles in the potholes so that his good solicitor's shoes and suit would not get splashed. Like any man who is in deep trouble, dealing with a man who seems to be in no trouble at all, I pitied myself. I marvelled at the sense of freedom he must feel, at his air of goodness. I felt I had a disease that he could never catch.

So, I'm trying here again to work out some other way of looking at this, some way of playing this game that feels better for me. I have to try to make myself feel better. I'm the only one who can do that, or who wants to do it.

But I can't do it right now: I have to kind of work myself into it, a bit like meditation. Later on maybe another three pints will do it for me, like last night.

I open a Word document on my laptop, and I call it 'John Devlin – A Statement'. I am also keeping a window on a few of the last races at Newbury and at Wolverhampton, to see if I can add to that ninety-euro profit or if I am back to all square.

I start to type.

> *My name is John Devlin, and in this document I will outline the full extent of the crimes I have committed, and I will attempt to express my deep remorse for what I have done.*

There have been many victims here, some of them close personal friends, from whom I took money under false pretences, and, of course, my wife, Christina, who is in her own way a victim of my addiction.

And that is the only explanation I can offer – I became addicted to gambling, then to lying and to dishonest dealing so that I could keep gambling, in order to maintain a lifestyle I had originally gained through gambling.

Regardless of what sentence I may be given, I would hope to use my time before I go to prison and also my time in prison to help others to understand the nature of this addiction, to stop gambling as I have finally stopped, with the help of counselling and the fellowship of Gamblers Anonymous, by seeking help from a Higher Power.

But for now, I throw myself on the mercy of the authorities, as someone who has fallen very low, who has thrown away everything in what I can only describe as a frenzy. A madness that took hold of me, and that has had such a traumatic effect on so many people around me . . .

I break off from the confessional there to note that I am now two hundred euro ahead on the day, which brings me the happy thought of another few drinks in the pub tonight. And I break off also because there's an alternative narrative that is better in truth than this official account, one that I can't allow into this statement, because being more honest ... it wouldn't do me any good. And it would be a disappointment to James Hamilton, who is now someone I don't want to disappoint – maybe, having disappointed everyone else who ever knew me, I feel like I need to hang on to him.

But I can't help thinking all the same – I can't help thinking, thinking, thinking – that the friends who gave me their money to invest were being a bit greedy. In fact, they were being exceptionally greedy. Because, as my friends, they knew deep down there was only ever one way that I made money, and that was by gambling.

They knew that I had paid for my time in university, and that I had lived a lot better than most students, mainly by playing poker. That I had put a large deposit on my first house out of a successful three days at Cheltenham. That for a long time I had been living on my wits, not on my wise investments.

They had this vague idea that I was making inspired calls of some kind – that I was some kind of a magician of the markets – but some at least must have known I was giving them those ridiculous returns on their money because I was essentially gambling. Maybe they didn't know exactly how I was gambling, on stocks and shares, on the online poker, on horses, on football, on golf, on baseball, even on fucking tennis, but they knew there was something strange about my operation.

They knew, but they didn't want to know. They wanted to believe in me, even if it didn't make sense. And when I was able to buy properties with the money I was taking in, and the money I was winning, they all went with that story – now that, along with my magical powers, I was able to say it was the real estate that was doing it. Now they could feel even better about it. Now they could rejoice in the expensive bottle of wine I was sending to their table.

I'd be muttering to them about property deals and land deals and just deals, deals, deals, and they'd be muttering to me about deals, and the muttering would reach another few people who would want a piece of this portfolio. They all liked that word, 'portfolio', as I recall. But in their hearts they must have known that the money I was giving back to them could not have been generated just by some portfolio, however sweet it sounded. For those beautiful percentages to keep racking up every year, it would need a little extra creativity on my part.

At various times I actually had properties in London, Manhattan and the south of France, and the more ammunition I had, the easier it tended to become – when you have more money to punt, you can punt it at more conservative odds. But even then you can lose sometimes. And then you need to dispose of some of that portfolio.

Christina would see me struggling on those bad nights. She would catch me utterly destroyed after I got back to the house from a long session on the screens, playing poker with some drunk in Vilnius, maybe starting to suspect that there could never be enough poker, or enough drunks in Vilnius, to make it right. She would be reading articles and hearing the odd professor warn that the thing might turn ugly – I have heard the boom described in a lot of ways but 'the thing' sounds just about right, spoken to me by a punter who was so exhausted by it all he couldn't find any expression other than 'the thing'. But Christina had a line that seemed to get her through those warnings about the thing: she figured we had so many houses in so many places, so much to sell, we could never possibly run out of money – and even if we were running low, we could hang on until all the other people who had run out of money wanted to buy houses again. She knew there was a hole somewhere in the story but she didn't want to know what it was. Because she was addicted just like them, just like me, addicted to the fix of the easy money and all the lovely things it could bring, the clothes, the cars, the apartment we had in Villefranche-sur-Mer.

It was at Villefranche that I knew for sure it would all go down. We were having a pizza and a Coke outside a café when I started talking about the Rolling Stones' connection with the place, something we had talked about many times, how they recorded *Exile On Main St* in Villefranche, in the Villa Nellcôte, and how I could still feel the spirit of Keith Richards and Anita Pallenberg, and all those fine people who hung out in the villa with them, in every breeze on this part of the Riviera. I could still hear the noise of the rock'n'roll, which was so loud it could be heard all around Villefranche, the noise that Pallenberg heard when she came down from the villa to the town during the day, and sometimes during the night. I could hear 'Tumbling Dice', the gambler's song.

It felt like I was talking to myself, not just because I had said all these things before, not because Christina didn't care about the Stones, because she did – she had a certain amount of taste in just about everything – but because in most situations at that time I felt like I was talking to myself, that I was retreating further each day into some zone in which there was nothing but me and all the money I was losing, irretrievable.

And there was so much that I could hardly even talk about to myself. That day while we were having lunch down the hill from our apartment on the Côte d'Azur, I was trying desperately to sell that apartment. I was waiting for a call about it, my heart sick with anxiety. But I wasn't telling Christina that: I was still telling her about Tom Waits describing *Exile On Main St* as 'a tree of life'. So I made an effort, in my way, by mentioning that the Stones were running out of money when they'd come here, but she didn't connect with what I was telling her.

'They got it back, though, didn't they?' she said.

That little note of optimism nearly broke me. I felt a surge of compassion for her, knowing all the things she didn't know but was about to find out. We were on our way back to the apartment when I got the call saying there was no deal, that the thing was fucked, that people were getting out of property, in fact people were getting out of everything. Which was leaving me with a load of desirable properties that nobody desired anymore, and a load of people starting to look for money that I didn't have anymore.

Yes, the Rolling Stones got it back, over time, but the Rolling Stones were great artists, who would always be able to raise a million as a kind of a moral entitlement, just by showing up somewhere, whereas hustlers like me thought we were so entitled without the art. We thought we had a claim on some infinite source of money that would materialise just from punting and from bullshitting.

And still I didn't tell Christina, because still I hoped that, somehow, I wouldn't have to. But I made another effort, in my way, as we strolled up the hill back to the apartment. I had just checked my phone to learn that a bet of fifty grand on the second favourite in the Irish Derby had gone down. I had been counting on that to keep one of my clients from breaking down the walls.

'As long as we have each other,' I said, as I turned off the phone.

But she just kept walking, as if I had said nothing, as if all that business I was doing on the phone was just my thing, a kind of a personal obsession with no real bearing on the great issues, as if I was still just rambling about the Stones. And looking at her that day, on that hill, which kept getting steeper, like some crude representation of all that we were facing, I understood that she didn't respond, that she maintained her denial, because she was made that way. She didn't have the imagination to see a time when she would be in a situation in which there was actually no money of any kind. She was just too middle class, to the core of her being, not equipped for any other kind of life, and I knew to the core of my being that when it all went down she would not be there with me.

I called that right.

So I am now in this grotesque caravan, I, who once owned a piece of Villefranche-sur-Mer, and all I can do is watch the game.

She is talking to journalists about the disgrace I have brought on her and on her family, who never really took to me in the first place, the distinguished bastards – indeed her father, who made his money running some insurance racket, has spoken of his one consolation: that there are no grandchildren with this stain on their name, that Christina is still young enough to start again with 'somebody who is decent'. Somebody, I take it, whose father was not a busman. I actually have a magazine in this caravan which contains that article, in which Christina adds that 'the one blessing' is that people are not blaming her, but that she blames herself anyway, such is her shame at the destruction I have wrought. But there wouldn't be such shame if she hadn't been getting herself into magazines in the first place with all her fucking bullshit. If she hadn't invited them into our home to take photographs of how graciously we were living.

I went along with it – I have no defence to that. It did not disturb me at the time because I had other things to be disturbed about, like the forty grand that went down on a game of cricket on the morning of a shoot, forty grand down, and there was Christina using the loveliness of our lives to promote some good cause – forty grand down and I'm talking to this photographer about the excellence of my portfolio.

It seems from this latest article that she is looking after herself now, that the only cause left to her, perhaps the most urgent of them all, is to put me down and warn the general public to stay away from me.

And, from this magazine, it is clear to me that her tragedy has made her more beautiful, given her some new dimension, a kind of indomitability, now that she has been liberated from the sickness I brought into her world. In fact, this terrible thing that has happened to her may be one of the few things that has ever happened to her that is not bullshit, by which I mean that it is true, and it is sad, and it is real, and it is profound, and some day she might even get around to putting a small bit of the blame for it on herself. I think it might make her a better person in the end and, if I am being completely honest, she was decent enough already. I can see her being played in the movie by a gutsy Reese Witherspoon, and I think there will be a movie, and I am sure that I will not be coming out of that one too well either.

I heard an old gambler once saying that you shouldn't expect too much of people, and since he happened to be a highly successful gambler, I paid attention to his little motto. I don't think he was being pessimistic: I think he meant that, if you don't expect too much, you can be pleasantly surprised.

So I guess I never really expected Christina to come with me if something went seriously wrong but, no, I have not been pleasantly surprised.

Her father, who really is a phenomenal asshole, is declaring that he always knew I was a wrong one, but that Christina was too good a person to see that. That I probably never loved her, that I couldn't have loved her, but I don't know about that either. I mean, really, I don't know. I loved someone when I was about sixteen, and it was different from whatever I felt for Christina, but I figured there was nothing wrong with that: it was bound to be more powerful the first time. Then again, by the time I met Christina no feeling for any person was as powerful as the feeling I would get when I came away from working the screens with more money than I had when I'd sat down. So, if her father wants to nail me for that one too, he is not completely wrong.

He's making it easy on himself, though, like all those people I used to know, giving themselves the benefit of every doubt. They've all agreed about how shocked they were to discover I was only running what they call a Ponzi scheme, and maybe they were shocked at the way it all went down in the end. Shocked that smart people like them could get burned just because they wanted a bit of an edge. But even the part about the Ponzi scheme isn't really true because, as far as I know, a Ponzi scheme is only a Ponzi scheme if the intention from the start is to shake everybody down. In fact my man James looked it up for me the other day, giving me the definition that 'a Ponzi scheme is a form of fraud in which belief in the success of a non-existent enterprise is fostered by the payment of quick returns to the first investors from money invested by later investors'.

My enterprises were never non-existent, though towards the end there were occasions when they weren't fully existent either, depending on the time of day or the result of the last race at Uttoxeter. It was only during those last days in Villefranche that my little operation finally started to look like a straightforward Ponzi scheme in the true sense, that I was faced with the task of stonewalling certain people, until they came banging at my front door, and getting money out of certain other people with a serious chance that they would never get it back, that I would just be passing those other people's money around as fast as I could, until the music stopped. But from the start I did not want anybody to lose, I wanted everybody to win, and for about nine years that was what happened. Contrary to the legend, I never went looking for mugs to finance my racket. It was the mugs who came looking for me. Because they'd heard I was good.

They didn't trouble themselves greatly with what exactly I was good at, they just knew that, whatever it was, I was good at it.

And maybe if they hadn't all come rushing for their money at the same time, I'd still be doing it. But with the thing going down, and everything else going down, they did come rushing. And when they found out that there wasn't really much going on in London, or Manhattan, or the south of France anymore, they became hysterical. And I couldn't stop them. I couldn't persuade them to keep calm, to wait for the magic to return, as I believe it would have done.

Ah, most surely it would have done. All I needed was time.

In fact, they mock me and despise me all the more because I told them I could turn it around, if they gave me the time.

So they are now the innocent, the abused, and I am the Ponzi Man.

I don't think that's fair, or right, and I figure that no well-rounded person would think it right either.

But the place I'm in, I won't be dealing with any of them.

A banger in the distance tells me that Hallowe'en is coming. It also gives me an urge to rise up again and go to the pub. It's only one noise in the distance but even that is enough to start a stirring in me, some sense that there's something out there, or maybe just the memory of something, some other Saturday night.

I put on my black Paul Smith coat, though I am aware that people are angry to see me still well-dressed, like I should burn all my old clothes in a display of my shame. I also have a good pair of handmade black shoes to go with it. And a dark brown cashmere jumper and a pair of jeans that must have cost about three hundred euro – Christina and I didn't really rate anything that cost less, and I've got to say that, despite all the changes and the damp in this caravan, the expensive stuff is still holding its shape. It has moved with me from a walk-in wardrobe that was roughly the size of my mobile home to this place of purgatory, and it is not diminished. It is all about the cut.

If these fine garments make me look defiantly prosperous, so much the better. I am actually enjoying the tease, the way that people look at me and think maybe I have a few million stashed away, just because I'm still wearing a rich man's clothes.

And, in my own mind, I have an image of various fellows who went to the bad and still dressed as if they were doing fine. Maybe it was my uncle Christy who started this for me, always wearing a suit as the whiskey consumed him, even on a hot Sunday as he was buying me a 99. But it was probably those seedy Anglo-Irish types who had the strongest influence in this regard – I was always impressed by the air of nonchalant delinquency they maintained through it all, though I could never quite match it. If you're not born with it, you will hear that little plebeian voice reminding you that you have done something disgraceful, and you will find it very hard to kill that voice.

But I am trying, and I think I am succeeding at that. I am learning that when they drive you to the sort of place that I'm in, to a caravan at the end of the world, in some way that they don't understand they start to lose their power over you. Maybe that's why I'm reluctant to go along with their desire for a full statement of the damage I did and the remorse I feel. It might be good for me but it's also good for them: it gives them the sense that they own my soul just as surely as they own my arse for the next few years.

The sound of another banger gets me out the door and hopping around the puddles, like James Hamilton. Hallowe'en I remember as a time of the deepest happiness. I would come up to the village on the mid-term break from school, and I would gorge myself on the television I could never see at home. Even then I was obsessed with time, trying to hang on to every moment, while knowing that each of those moments was bringing me closer to the end of this perfect state.

Still the memory of being able to watch *The Old Grey Whistle Test* and *Top of the Pops*, on those Hallowe'en nights, pierces me to the core. With the summer gone, there was no 'Young Girl' pumping out of the amusements anymore, but there was Springsteen on *Whistle Test* chasing something that he had heard in the great music of America, because the life that was handed to him wasn't good enough, and there was me looking deep into that screen chasing something I couldn't even name, and starting out from a place three thousand miles behind Springsteen, and here I am tonight wanting crazily to be back there again, with some kind of a life to look forward to, maybe calling around to one of the guys in the band – not Ed in this case, but the keyboard player, name of Aidan – who in my mind is forever with me listening to *Stupidity*, the Dr Feelgood live album, on the small speakers of the stereo in his bedroom, familiar enough with it to be playing the imaginary drums in imitation of The Big Figure. Or maybe just in imitation of Ed.

I think it was the sound of the crowd on that album that I loved, nearly as much as the sound of the band, the notion that there was this tribe of people in England, or wherever the Feelgoods were playing, who knew the greatness of the band, who had worked it out for themselves, who stood there together in large numbers in the halls where the album had been recorded, not in little groups of two or three, like Aidan and Ed and me. Yet we were out here, too: we were a part of this thing. I remember walking home alone from Aidan's house that night, on a dark road leading into the village, feeling that I understood what people mean when they say they are at one with the world. And knowing that this, too, would get away from me. That even a minor dislocation from this feeling of unity would leave me about three hundred years away from where I needed to be. That soon the elation of a walk in the dark with the people of this tribe all walking with me, all of us wired to the one thing, would be replaced by what I knew better, a feeling that I was on the outside of everything.

Aidan, Ed, the people they knew, were not on the outside, it seemed to me. But one of them at least has eventually got there, and now he wants to meet me.

The thought of it gives me a burst of nervous energy. As I hurry down the village towards Cooney's, I am tempted to walk past the pub and to keep on walking until I get to Ed's house, to go there and talk with him into the night, like we used to do.

But I think I will drink first. I will have my three pints and more, more than that, and I might even get a bit drunk, because it's one of the last Saturday nights I'll be having for a while. And when I come out this door at Cooney's around closing time, then I will decide.

CHAPTER 5

He says he can't serve me. This barman, who is about twenty-five, wearing a white shirt and a black tie, tells me quietly he can't serve me.

So I ask him why, and he just says he's sorry, he can't serve me. I say that the barman here last night served me, but he ignores me, taking an empty glass off the counter and throwing it into the sink.

It is about eight, just before the evening crowd arrives, and there is one other customer in the bar, in the seat where I was sitting last night, with another in the lounge, behind his newspaper. They are paying no attention to us.

For a moment I have an urge to ring my solicitor, and in

the next I realise that this would be ridiculous. I am also a bit embarrassed to take out my phone, a cheap pay-as-you-go type, a builder's phone. I figure that the barman would take note of the primitive piece and would despise me just a little bit more, so I deny him that feeling of superiority. Such are the small vanities that remain with me.

'Was it the singing?' I say, trying to strike a light-hearted tone, remembering what James had told me about his talk with the sergeant.

The barman turns his back on me and starts rearranging bottles of Guinness on the shelves. People think they can just turn their backs on me now without explanation. If it was the singing, then I have given them a handy excuse. What the barman doesn't know is that he has an even better excuse – that this is karma: I was due this blow for all the barmen and waiters to whom I spoke in the wrong way. Yes, it is karma, and I accept it.

My situation has clarified so many things for me, one of which is the casual cruelty of people, how they will put you down if they can, even when you're already down. How they find it so hard to be kind to the likes of me probably, I think, because they're afraid. They know at some level that what has happened to me could happen to them, if they get a bad break. So they push it away, searching for some sense of security in those attitudes of disdain, those miserable little displays of self-righteousness. And, unlike me with my over-tipping, they don't feel the need to make amends.

They are all separating themselves from me now, all except James Hamilton, for whom being an associate of mine is a job.

I walk out of the bar, with no further argument, like it's no big deal to me. But it has shaken me, this latest rejection.

I realise that the people who used to run Cooney's are all gone now, that this new crowd feels no connection to me, no need even to sell me a drink just for old times' sake, and maybe that's the part that hurts – I was here before these people.

I cross the road to the promenade and sit on the wall, looking across the bay at the lights on the mountains. The scenery never meant much to me, maybe because I grew up with it, but tonight it seems to be bringing on a touch of sadness in me. I remember the night my mother came out of our place when they were taking her to be treated for cancer, and she stopped for a few minutes to have a long look at this view that I am looking at now, as if she knew she would never see it again.

Maybe it has stuck in my head because she was never the sentimental type. Because I was surprised she gave a damn about the view, about those lights over there in the houses of strangers, just as I am now surprised at myself, and the sadness that has got into me.

It was she who had some old family connection with this place, who brought us up here, and yet the first time I saw her show some emotion towards it was when she was seeing it for the last time. Or maybe she was seeing something else, like a mother dying at the age of forty-two, leaving a boy of seventeen. Maybe, like me, it took her too long to appreciate the true nature of things – she thought she knew things without really knowing them at all – and maybe this is why I am feeling this sadness, for her and for myself, realising at this moment that she lived in her head as much as I do, and stood back from things, and people, rather than embrace them. I guess she knew, best of all, that my father had married the wrong woman.

I didn't know any such thing. I just knew there was something wrong in the whole arrangement because when I went to other people's houses I felt there was something essentially different going on there, something better. And I don't think it was just the fixtures and the fittings.

It is an unusually warm October, no small thing for a man who is spending a lot of his time in a damp mobile home with one gas heater. I am looking across the water to the lights on the other side of the bay, but I'm thinking of all the people who used to be here for different reasons.

Before the amusements were established in the building next to Cooney's, they had amusements on the beach here every summer, with slot machines and stalls and swinging boats – I can see the boss man at the boats with a little leather bag full of money similar to the ones the bus conductors used to have, an image that has remained with me like that vision of Walter Jackson's bookie's satchel and the treasure it contained. I became obsessed with one attraction in particular, a roll-a-penny game, which seemed to work for me, which seemed in my imagination like something from a fairground in an English comic. I can see this other machine that I liked because it was just a beautiful thing, with a silver ball that you would send shooting around the glass case until it dropped into the right pocket or not, and I can see all those sunburned Northerners sitting along the promenade eating bags of chips and ice-creams with the swinging boats rising and falling behind them.

Right here, against this wall, there was a stall every Sunday, at which you could buy a ticket and win prizes on the spin of a wheel. It was run by these mad old women to raise money for the parish. And there was a time when I used to try to please my mother by buying tickets to win some kind of ornament or a clock or a canteen of cutlery that I could present to her. Which sounds very big-hearted of me, except that I was using coins I'd stolen from various jars and windowsills around the house to buy the tickets.

And time after time they would spin the wheel, and the noise of it would cause this childish sense of excitement to build, but somehow it never stopped at my number. I could not believe my bad luck back then, and I still can't believe it. But I would keep trying anyway, imagining the moment when I could present my mother with some china dog, demented with longing for that feeling of achievement.

If I ever get to sit down with one of those counsellors that

James Hamilton wants me to see, and I tell them about it, they won't have to go digging very deep after that. It's about gambling – it's about gambling with someone else's money, it's about stealing, it's about a juvenile need to please, and at the end of it there is utter failure.

It's all there, so completely that I am inclined to dismiss it. It may seem as if the entire pattern of my life was established on those desperate Sundays, but I have studied a few patterns myself over the years, in a professional way, and the only thing I know for sure about them is that they can fool you. That you think you've got it nailed down right up until the very moment you realise it's all going to change.

And there is one slight difference between those adolescent efforts of mine, and the story of the rest of my life. When I was a kid, I didn't get found out.

Or maybe I did get found out, and they just let me away with it. Which now seems like a pretty serious mistake on their part, all things considered.

Or maybe it was just bad luck and nothing else. We prefer to find reasons, and people to blame, because the alternative is to put it all down to a few bad breaks, which is too frightening. Maybe thirty years ago if I had won just once, on the spin of that fucking wheel, it would have been the break that changed things for me.

It's a thing I have noticed about my own gambling, that when I have a substantial win I can lose interest for a little while. It's as if I am satisfied that I was right all along. And the desire recedes in me.

But when I am losing, I can never rest.

'They even served me . . .'

The voice behind me makes me jump a little. It takes me a moment to establish two things about the speaker, the first that he is probably the man who was sitting in the other part of Cooney's, the lounge, mostly hidden by the newspaper he was reading, and the second that he is Ed Brennan. In certain ways he is unrecognisable and yet I recognised him straight away, which doesn't make sense, but then I'm not expecting that anymore.

He lights a cigarette, which illuminates his face, his smile like that of Tony Soprano being nice. Ed usen't to smoke, but then he usen't to drink much either. He joins me on the wall, sitting down beside me. We shake hands, warmly, automatically. I am still taking him in, the largeness that doesn't seem so large to me now, the receding hair that may be dyed brown, the neatness of his jeans and his leather jacket and his sharp-looking boots, which were all features of the Ed I knew. But his face seems to have been blasted with the red blotches that are usually the mark of the drinker.

'Ed . . .' I say.

'Johnny . . .'

He alone used to call me Johnny. With everyone else it was John.

'Ed . . . I'm sorry I didn't know it was you . . . in the pub.'

'You sure it's me now?'

I lean back a bit theatrically to study him, getting past the superficial features and the clothes reeking of cigarettes to feel that there is still an intensity that comes from the man, from that big head and that powerful body, remembering that Ed was one of the first people I knew who could put on a really strong display of what the therapists call passive-aggressive behaviour. I sense he still has that strength, that if anything he seems more aggressive. But eventually I am seeing only the blotches, and trying not to see them. I decide to flatter him. 'About ninety-five per cent sure, which is very, very good,' I say.

'Thanks, Johnny, you charming bastard.'

Johnny . . . again, it takes a moment for this to register after years of John. He makes his own assessment of me, observing me with amusement.

'I was thinking of coming down to you tonight,' I say.

He is still making his assessment. 'Still all the same hair, the same face . . . you're fine,' he says.

I realised when I was about twenty-one that I'd always looked fine, or fine enough at any rate, but that was just another of those things I didn't know when I needed to know it, when I was younger. 'I'm hearing this terrible shit about you,' I say.

The line is out of my mouth almost without my thinking, the sort of crack I might have made to Ed a lifetime ago, saying the wrong thing and not caring about it, sitting up late together drinking vodka and white lemonade on the quiet until we were out of our minds, dreaming the same dream.

'Slander. It comes with success,' he says.

I think he is engaging in self-deprecation here but I am not entirely sure. He says it straight, and leaves it there.

'It comes with failure too,' I say.

Those blotches are not good. As we sit on the wall with the tide coming in, talking as if we had just resumed a conversation we were having a long time ago, the marks of maybe twenty years of alcoholism are the one part of Ed that seems radically different because Ed always looked right, he would be buying clothes and getting a decent haircut every few weeks. He would shudder in his superior way at various errors of style that he encountered on the streets of the town, secure in the soundness of his own taste. I learned a lot from Ed in that way.

He runs through a list of some of the people we knew, and what happened to them. Danny works for an advertising agency in London. Joanne is a solicitor. Paul is running a hotel somewhere in the North. Catherine has some kind of a child-minding business in the town. They all sound very settled. Like they grew up, leaving the two of us wasters here, waiting for the end.

For a moment, neither of us has anything to say, as if all the things that are too hard to say have caused an obstruction.

All we hear is the sea, the sound I used to hear in my bed at night, without really hearing it at all.

'Annie Campbell . . . she's gone too,' he says, sucking on a new cigarette.

'Gone?'

'Canada.'

I make some sort of acknowledgement. And I mention a couple of others I can think of, trying to imagine them now as middle-aged teachers and civil servants, but seeing them only at some party on a summer evening at which the music is always *Rumours*.

Annie Campbell is gone too. He hit me with that and I think he knows he hit me. Annie Campbell was the girl I loved when I was sixteen or seventeen, and Ed knew that at the time. He brings her name up now in exactly the way he used to, with a hint in his voice. For a moment I lose my bearings, because he is making me think about her again, making me feel connected to this episode of my youth. Making me feel all that stuff I could never quite feel for Christina.

I loved Annie, but I can't say she ever loved me because we never did much about it.

We just wrote letters to one another.

I was living during the school year in the midlands, meeting her occasionally at weekends in the village. Not meeting *her* specifically, just meeting her with a lot of the others and talking to her and being petrified.

Only in the letters could we express ourselves with some

freedom, and then it was mainly me showing off how smart I could be, and her replying in admiring tones about what a hilarious guy I was indeed. But her letters were as long as mine, four or five pages, so she clearly had some interest in me. I can put it no stronger than that.

I can't really remember what we wrote about, just everyday stuff, but I remember the feeling I used to get when those letters from her would arrive, and I guess it was so strong and so pure because it never went beyond that, much though I wanted it to. She was one of those girls who didn't make as much of herself as she might. Maybe because she felt she didn't need to, which was attractive in itself. She had brown eyes, which tend to make me nervous, and brown hair, which mustn't have made an impression on me because I couldn't tell you now if it was long or short, maybe something in between. And she was tall, with a slightly loping walk. She had high cheekbones, great cheekbones; she had this elegance.

I managed to ask her to go to the pictures, how I do not know. Perhaps the trauma of it has erased the actual circumstances, though I think I must have phoned her, from our home telephone in the hall, when no one else was listening. And so we ended up one night in the town, with snow on the ground and Elvis's *Blue Hawaii* showing for some reason that has always escaped me. And I froze. I could not touch her.

These are the extremes that I remember, the exhilaration

of the letters and the blankness of the reality, of being able to express myself to her in ink but not in person. Of my body refusing to carry out the most basic instructions. And of her just letting it pass, the moment, the night, whatever it was.

Which made me believe she wasn't really on for it anyway, that to her I was just a pen pal, the saddest of all sad things it seems to me now. At least, that is what I wanted to believe. I could see no reason why anyone would want to be with me anyway, which reinforced that belief.

But I see it now not just as a mark of my inadequacy but as a sign that I really was different. That I didn't have the same facility as my friends for just getting on with people, and getting off with them, but I had this other way of turning the game in my direction, and I was starting to become aware of it, this gambling thing. And intuitively I protected it: I knew that I could never allow what they call a relationship to consume my attention. Around that time I had started to spend afternoons in a betting office in the town, wanting to be down in that cave with those tormented men, loving the idea that I needed nobody else for this. It would be just me, against the elements, against the gods, and I would win.

And soon Annie, like all the others, had drifted into actual relationships, with guys who knew what they were doing in that line, but not with Ed himself – she was one of the few Ed did not have.

'What's Annie doing?' I say.

He decides to take the piss. 'What do you think she's

doing, Johnny?' He gives me a kind of dirty smile, as if he's about to tell me that she's coming back from Canada to be the madam of this drunken whorehouse he is rumoured to be running, or maybe that he is not running at all.

'Just tell me, Ed.'

He considers this for a while, as if it's complicated. 'I'll give you a clue. I'd say that what she does is the opposite of what I do.'

'But what is it that you do, Ed?'

'Ah . . . I don't do anything really. I just live . . . you know? I just live, that's all I do . . . live.'

'So, she stops people living.'

'In a kind of a way, yes.'

'You're not helping me much here, Ed.'

He throws his head back and laughs, showing no desire to dispute this. 'Keep going,' he says.

'Is she some kind of a psychiatrist, counsellor, a nurse, that sort of thing?' I say.

'Put it like this. What she does is probably the opposite of what you do too.'

'She's . . . a bookie?'

'I'll tell you what she is, Johnny. She's a police inspector.'

'Oh, for fuck's sake.'

I invite him up to my place and he accepts. I was kind of expecting him to dismiss the offer and to invite me down to his place instead since it is, after all, a house, not a shack sitting on cement blocks. And because we spent so many Saturday nights down there, it still seems like the natural destination, even after all this time. But it's much further to walk to his place than to mine, so in that respect the old caravan makes sense. And when he heads over to Cooney's to get two bottles of gin, and several bottles of tonic, and a bag of ice, and more cigarettes, that makes sense too – at the height of my own drinking, I wouldn't walk an extra mile with that thirst on me, just to get to my favourite chair.

I, too, am in the mood for drinking. I am intoxicated already by our meeting, by having a conversation with someone who knew me before I was the Ponzi Man. And by the two-way thing that is going on here, talking to Ed as he is tonight, and talking also to some version of him that has existed in my mind since we were kids.

We are walking up the promenade towards my place, but I am still seeing him getting the tables ready in his father's pub while I sit on a high stool at the counter listening to the PA system, which is playing the first track on Bob Dylan's *Street Legal*, which Ed has just brought back from the North. I see him arranging the beer mats and I hear Dylan's band striking up the opening bars of 'The Changing Of The Guard', remembering how it made us feel to have that record ahead of everyone we knew.

I am wondering, too, what Annie Campbell thinks of me, or if she thinks of me at all. Ed's description has taken her out of the land of youth and into the hard reality of the present. Given what she does for a living, and the kind of person I became, I am doubting we ever had a chance, which is comforting to me, but I wonder if she knows about my fall, and I wonder what she feels about that. I wonder, and then I stop my wondering because it pains me, and then I start wondering again.

I don't really feel much shame at the thought that she knows how I have turned out, what I have done. I guess I see someone in her position having a professional understanding of these things. Or maybe guys like me have just run out of shame.

And I am not totally surprised by what she is doing, mainly because I never really imagined her doing anything after I drifted away from this place. I had lost interest by then: she was gone, we were both gone.

I'm not even surprised that she has risen so high in the police because, as it happened, I was arrested and cautioned by a female officer, and I have actually found my dealings with the force not unpleasant, now that they tend to come across as social workers who unfortunately have the power to send you to jail for seven years. Which I think is what I will get.

Seven years, both for the egregious nature of my fraudulent activities, and because nearly everyone else got away with whatever they did during the thing, so they want to get the most out of me. And because I am so far gone I am not doing the things that James Hamilton is asking me to do.

As I tell Ed, when we skip through the puddles, I have been fighting hard to keep thoughts of jail out of my head.

'I can't think about jail for more than five seconds since this all started,' I say, pushing open the unlocked door of the caravan and making quickly for the Super Ser.

'That's good,' he says, making for the presses to take out two glasses for the gin.

'Such is my terror.'

'Denial . . . denial is good,' he says.

'Such terror . . . I don't even lock the door of this place in case it puts the thought of a prison cell in my head.'

'Try this,' he says, handing me a full tumbler of Gordon's and Schweppes and ice, the drops of sweat starting to pop out on his forehead as the blue flame burns, and the front panels of the heater change from white to red. Gin is not my regular drink but it feels right for this place, reminding me strangely of the government gin that Winston Smith was drinking in *1984*, the pure badness of it seeming to complement the godforsaken cruelty of the living conditions.

I'm guessing that maybe for Ed it's as much about the tonic as the gin, that the mixer allows him to drown the booze and therefore to swallow more of it all round than might be the case with whiskey or brandy – and I note that he can live without the slice of lemon.

We drag the heater down into the main part of the caravan, so that we can stretch out on the seats. There are nights when I look at this interior and it reminds me very much of a very large coffin, but I don't share this with Ed.

We are about to drink when he reaches across the little

table between us and holds my hand. He grips it tightly. 'Here's to Johnny Devlin, the only man around here who made a name for himself,' he says.

I can feel a powerful affection coming from him, and it's not the sentimental kind that comes from the bottle – I'm assuming that will come later.

We take our first gulps of the gin together, shuddering as it goes through us, all the way. In this glorious moment, I know for sure that we are going to get shatteringly drunk.

CHAPTER 6

E d reckons that the hardest part for me must have been the taxi-driving. We are getting through the first bottle of Gordon's fast, with Ed already lamenting his lack of foresight in not getting three bottles, four. But he figures he's right about the taxi-driving and I don't dispute it.

I still find it hard to select one particular aspect of my fall as being the worst, but the few weeks in which I was driving a cab were definitely not good. Ed saw a picture of me taken without my knowledge for a Sunday paper, opening the back door for my passenger, and he felt such pity for me, he says, he almost cried. Now the memory of it is actually making him cry, or something like it. A kind of a snuffling, and a heaving of the shoulders, then another smoke and another drink.

He offers me a cigarette, a Rothmans, same as he always smoked, and with an old impulse I refuse it, and then with a new impulse – ah, fuck it – I accept it and he lights it for me and I start to smoke again after about fifteen years off them. That first drag might as well be a blast of opium, like the first Carrolls Number 1 I smoked at the side of the amusements. I try to get my bearings as Ed continues to commiserate about the taxi-driving.

I suppose the sad thing was not the taxi-driving itself, but the fact that I used to own the taxi company and, when it all went down for me, I had about 350 euro in cash to live on, maybe for the rest of my life, with everything else frozen.

Christina could get money from her parents so she could continue to live in the great house from which I was now barred, a contaminated presence in that and in any other decent neighbourhood.

So I sat down in the park one day, thinking it all through, a homeless man, and I decided that the thing I needed the most was a car. I couldn't afford rent, and I just wouldn't be safe walking the streets now that I was the Ponzi Man. I couldn't get away from the city at that time due to my ongoing dealings with members of the Fraud Squad, and I couldn't leave the country because they'd taken my passport and left me with nothing but the few bob on the Laser card after freezing about seven thousand they discovered in a long-forgotten bank account – forgotten by me anyway. Which pained me greatly because of course if I'd known it was still there, I could have used that money for gambling.

So I figured a car would do all the usual things that a car does but in my case it would also be a kind of a mobile home before eventually I moved to this more spacious version. And as the former owner of a taxi company, I knew where a car might be found.

The new owner was a man I first met during the thing when Ireland was so high on the improbability of it all, nobody could imagine some future time when it might so wearily be called 'the thing'. We were guests in an executive box at the Curragh, and I gave him a few winners that day, but then, I gave a lot of other people a winner here and a winner there, and I don't see many of them coming to me these days with offers of assistance, however humiliating – and dear God this was humiliating but it was still a big Lexus, in return for which I would pick people up from the airport and drive them into town. People with foreign names, who might not have heard of me. The new owner himself was called Buczek, not Irish enough yet to truly ostracise me.

A man's life gets complicated when he has no money. Maybe even as complicated, I found, as when he has money. Now I was calling in favours from a hotel porter who would let me use a room in a zombie hotel to take a shower and maybe to sleep for a night when I needed a break from sleeping in the car. I couldn't give him any money but I had over-tipped him a few times when I had it, and he was good enough to reciprocate. I was one of the few big losers of the time who really didn't have any money hidden out there. Which is something Ed doesn't really believe but he doesn't push me on it, concentrating instead on the deeper character flaws he saw in me from the start.

'You never stayed with anything, that's the big one. You never stayed with anything . . . or anyone. I mean, you got bored too easily. You had no tolerance or patience. You're such a smart fuck . . . but there's something wrong with you,' he says, opening the second bottle of gin.

I realise he is a bit more drunk than I am, that he probably had a few on board already when we met. But though his words are harsh, in my own drunkenness I am trying to accept that he is trying to help me. And in his derangement he is striking a few notes that I recognise. I have walked away from a lot of things at the first sign of unpleasantness. I have left a lot of parties early, and not always for the right reasons.

'I kept hearing these stories about you. You had a hundred girlfriends, you had a hundred houses, and they were good girlfriends, and good houses, but you were like a butterfly. You never stayed with anything,' he says, hammering away at his theme. I am sitting on the back window seat and he is standing over me, emphasising the authority he has taken upon himself.

'I had no girlfriends at all until I was about twenty,' I say, a soft defence.

'Well, from what I hear, you made up for it then, you fucker. One after another, one after another . . .'

I feel like explaining to him the nature of the gambler in these situations, how we regard women essentially as distractions from our sacred mission, that we can tolerate them as a kind of decoration but we don't really want to know them. Yes, I could tell him that, but it would feel like giving in completely.

'I was married to the same woman for five years. I stayed with her. If I never stayed with anyone, how could I stay with her?' I say.

He heads for the toilet, but then he stops to make another point. 'She's the one you shouldn't have stayed with,' he says.

He knows he's caught me with that.

Ed stands there with a triumphant little grin, happy enough to suspend that trip to the toilet for another little while.

'You know I'm right, don't you?' he says.

'You've got me there,' I say.

'Annie Campbell . . .' he says, like he's going to start again on Annie, pushing home his advantage.

'Please,' I say, holding up my hand to get him to stop talking, a reflex that comes from some feeling I cannot name because I don't really have the names for feelings anymore, not after about twenty years of trying to stay calm through all the winning and the losing, a lifetime of detachment in the service of the cause.

Whatever I choose to call it, Ed seems to have got it going in me, and I think he knows it, because he doesn't say whatever he was going to say about Annie.

He sweeps off to the toilet, giving me a while to compose myself. I should not be feeling this but I do, this ache in the gut that I really do not need, something else to be regretting, maybe the worst of them all, if I think about it too hard.

I light another cigarette. I go to the kitchen sink to dilute the gin with more tonic, fearing that the spirit is burning my insides or maybe just to make it last longer.

I take a gulp of the drink and it starts to work. It straightens this thing out in my head. It was not all down to me that nothing ever happened with Annie. I wrote all those letters; I gave it a chance. I froze on that night but just about every adolescent who has ever lived, with the exception of Ed Brennan, has done that. Annie was not exactly a neutral observer: she could have made it easier but she didn't, as I remember it. Probably because she didn't want to, it didn't mean that much to her, and if you mentioned my name to her now she would hardly recall even what I looked like. To her I have become one of many, some vague complication she encountered back then.

It was just an even-money shot that went down, and even-money shots go down forty times a day. So if I've got this feeling, I shouldn't have it. I have plenty of other things to be sad about, things that are mostly my fault. It's the fact that it's come on top of everything else that grieves me, in itself it was just something I lost that a million other kids have lost in roughly the same way because that is how we do things in this world. It was not the one that got away from me, just the one that got away from me on that night, which was like many other nights and, you know, I have had some winners too – I had a lot of winners.

So Ed is not right, not quite, because he still thinks I care about these failures with women, or he's implying that I should care, when what I really care about is that most games of online roulette are rigged, and that I even know how they're rigged, yet I still can't stop myself wanting to play them. That's one of the things I care most deeply about.

Ed comes staggering back to me, like a man trying to keep his balance in the aisle of a train. He sits down beside me and hugs me awkwardly; some of the sweat on his forehead gets onto mine. 'You'll rise again, Johnny,' he says.

'Look, Ed, it's not as if I'm presenting myself to you here as some sort of a fine human being. You don't need to tell me all the things that are wrong with me. I know,' I say.

He stops me there. 'You don't fucking know, that's the problem. You never thought you were wrong, you thought you were right. You're one of those assholes – assholes! – who think they're right all the time.'

'We were both like that, Ed,' I say.

'You were the worst,' he says.

I can't answer that so I am quiet for a minute, enjoying the gin and the cigarette. I'm thinking that maybe it is Ed's own disease that is leading him towards the truth about my gambling – gambling is about a lot of things but in the end it's about being proved right.

'You're right, Ed,' I say.

'Annie Campbell . . . Jesus . . .' he says, unable to let it go.

'So I fucked it up, I was . . .'

He sits down beside me and he sighs. 'An eejit, Johnny?' he says quietly, as if it pains him. As if by framing it as a question he's asking for my consent. Because we both know that in our world, in the demonology we shared, there was nothing worse than being an eejit, no condition more incurable. To the outsider an eejit might not seem like the worst thing you could call someone, but in our private language, however we arrived at it over time, it was maybe the lowest thing you could be. It was worse than being an asshole because you knew you were being an asshole, whereas the tragedy of the eejit was that he had no idea he was an eejit, and most of the time he thought he was a great fellow.

'Can we just round it all up and leave it at asshole?' I say.

He considers this, like a tyrant wondering if he should be merciful. 'Let's leave it there so for the time being . . . asshole,' he says.

'Thanks,' I say.

'So now you see it,' he says, as if he had been with me and supporting me through all the years and had finally broken through my defences.

'Looks like I let you down as well,' I say.

As regards my other faults, Ed is less confrontational. He is more the tough but warm-hearted older brother, remembering wryly all the trouble I brought upon him, like the way I would say the wrong thing to people.

We were trying to get a residency for the band in this lounge in the town, talking to the owner and his son about all the arrangements, when I mentioned to the owner that there was a rumour about him and the son having these IRA connections.

'It was like you just forgot he was there. Or you just didn't see him,' Ed says.

'I'd lay the blame on him for that. For being so fucking boring I was no longer conscious of his presence,' I say.

'Right. And because it was the truth,' he says.

'I actually worked hard over the years to stop myself doing it. If I was with someone like that I'd try to stop my mind drifting, to stay alert, like when you're driving in the rain.'

'You know we got that gig in the end?'

'Yeah, I think we did.'

'After saying the totally wrong thing, you managed to say the right thing, whatever it was, and you said it in some charming way. Probably sent the guy a handwritten note with nothing about the IRA in it, saying what a pleasure it had been to meet him and also his fine son.'

'And the best of luck with the bombing.'

Ed lets out a gurgling laugh, like he is trying not to laugh but can't help himself, and I recognise that laugh: it is his original laugh, the authentic laugh of Ed Brennan from long ago. I am laughing with him and it feels like I own it too, this laugh of mine that I generally don't have much use for anymore.

I am getting drunker but Ed is not looking much better. The blotches are so disturbing because they are set against the corpse-like paleness of the rest of his face and the jaundiced tint of his eyes. But his energy is still pumping, even if it is being boosted by the gin – you could imagine people being afraid of him.

'I know you well . . . knew you'd make it,' he says, jabbing his finger at me.

'And did you know what would happen in the end?'

He sits with this for a minute, drinking on it, as if some silence would show a certain amount of respect for my predicament.

'I was just surprised you kept it going for so long. All that success, all that popularity, everything going so well. Even looking at your picture in the paper, smiling your arse off, I could sense you were getting restless.'

'You do know me well.'

'I have taken a keen interest in your career.'

I've been warming up for this moment and I sense an opening. 'And, ah . . . yourself?' I say.

'Thank you for asking . . . was wondering when we were going to get off the fascinating subject of you,' he says.

'Fire away,' I say.

'You see me in front of you.'

'Yes.'

'And if you want to know how I got to be the way I am, I would say that about ninety-eight per cent of it was this . . .' He holds up his glass of sparkling gin, looking at it in a non-judgemental way.

'You didn't drink much back then.'

'I hadn't discovered it.'

'You were happy.'

He lets out a growl of frustration. 'I'm surprised at you in particular that you fell for that one. I was never happy growing up.'

'You hid it well.'

'The older I get, the more I admire my young self for the character I showed at times . . . the restraint.'

'But all the girlfriends . . .'

'I was good at all that. I had a kind of a talent for it. But it wasn't the talent I wanted to have. You know what I mean?'

'Like, you just put up with them?'

'Funny as it sounds, man, it was a bit like that.'

'Didn't look like it.'

'I didn't really know myself, you see. It was only later I learned to accept that I don't really want to have much to do with those people. Those good burghers, you know? They were not my kind.'

'You had it too easy.'

'Nah, I had it hard, Johnny, I had it hard. I was all wound up for a very long time. I was pretending to be somebody I wasn't, and then one day, one day . . . I just let myself go.'

'Ah, Jesus . . .'

He pours himself another drink, as if to demonstrate. He downs it. 'Now that . . . that wasn't hard.'

I start laughing at him. I can't help it. But he takes no offence, laughing along.

'You found yourself,' I say.

'And now I am that most rare of things . . . most rare. I am a truly happy drunkard,' he says.

He says it not in a defiant way, but with an air of real contentment, this truly happy drunkard drinking another night away. I have not seen many visions of true happiness, but I sense they shouldn't look like this.

'But maybe you'll find out eventually that you're not really happy at that either,' I say.

'Nah, this is the one. This is the life that suits me. It's not the best for my health, I'll grant you that, but for my soul it's . . . just right.'

Through the roaring of the booze I recall that I have known such men, not many, but a few who can drink themselves to death at an unforced pace, without the conventional worries that would visit most of us in that situation, without being troubled by the notion that it might be a bad idea. 'How I envy you,' I say.

He considers this. 'It's all right to be fucked up, you know, as long as . . . as long as you don't mind it.'

'Right.'

'And I think the one small difference between me and you is that you do mind it. For all your fucking trickery, at the end of it you have this thing called a conscience. You might deny it but you have one. I can feel it . . . can smell it.'

'That's the drunkard talking, Ed.'

'We should get back together,' he says. And he hands me another cigarette.

I can see myself now scrounging cigarettes in prison and being stabbed because of it. But I can't figure him out here, this shit about getting back together. My impression is that he's just bullshitting, saying something he thinks will make me feel better but which obviously doesn't mean anything, seeing as how I'm going to be away for some time. 'We could do great things. I just have no idea what they might be,' I say.

'Just living . . . just living. Is that not enough?'

'And what would we be living on?' I say, trying to edge him closer to some vague description of what badness he is engaged in.

Then he leans towards me and lowers his voice, as if anyone could be listening. 'I've got money . . . and you can turn it into more money.'

I look at him, wondering if some punchline is coming. He seems completely sincere, which again I am inclined to attribute to the drink.

Yet he is saying, in his gin-twisted way, that he believes in me, and I haven't heard anything like that for a long time.

I find it kinda funny but I also find it touching. 'Thanks, Ed, but after seven years in jail I probably won't be much good for anything.'

He falls into silence for a few moments, as if making a careful assessment. 'Have you no cards to play?'

He leaves it hanging there, like it's a puzzle he's setting for me, and I, with my famous instincts for making the right calls, will somehow guess the right answer. I am trying to figure out what he means, feeling that if I crack this it will be a triumph in itself.

Now I'm tired of the drunken guessing. 'Cards to play? I'm not even allowed within five miles of the fucking casino.'

He pauses, as if this will be worth the wait. 'At the risk of repeating myself, I've got money . . . and you could turn it into a lot more money.'

'You mean, without going to jail first?'

'Say you paid back some of the money that you stole . . .'

'But I have no money,' I say, as if I am talking to a child.

'But, like I said, I have.'

'Right . . . you have money.'

'And if you could magic up a bit more . . .'

Again I feel this lethal dart of hope, and I can't take it. 'The magic is gone, Ed.'

He nods in reluctant acceptance that I am too fragile tonight for such big talk. But in my fragility I am slowly starting to acknowledge that what he says is not totally without foundation. If I could raise a lot of money in the next fortnight, a few hundred grand, perhaps, to pay back something to the two people who have actually made sworn statements against me, I guess there is a chance that it might influence the judge – most of my clients to whom I owe hundreds of thousands will not be there, wishing to avoid further grief and embarrassment and, maybe, a few questions about their unorthodox portfolio arrangements.

In theory, playing with someone else's money, the someone else in this case being Ed, a man of my abilities could at least conceive of such a result. Yes, in theory, and maybe even in practice too. I once made about half a million over a weekend, when a crazy series of results came in for me. I have seen such things happen in this world. But the thought of it, vaguely within reach but probably not going to happen now, is already starting to break my heart just another little bit. And Ed, even at such a late hour, seems sensitive to this.

'I'll tell you something else so . . . I know about forty people in this town, and I mean at least forty, who are in the shit too. Some of it worse that your shit,' he says.

He is still trying to make me feel better, in his way.

'I'm delighted to hear that,' I say.

'Very deep shit indeed,' he says.

'Talking about yourself again . . . friends of yours?'

He drains the last of the gin. 'No, I'm talking about the good burghers,' he says.

It is deep into the night, getting on for morning. He

stands up and starts to lose balance. I catch him just as he is falling over, just before he does great damage to my little table. He grips my hand again, this time to steady himself. But dizziness seems to get the better of him again, and this time he is dragging me down with him.

We make the caravan shake as we hit the floor, and by the time I extricate myself from his grip he is in a dead sleep.

CHAPTER 7

I must have drifted into unconsciousness too. Not sleep, you couldn't call it sleep. I am brought out of it by James Hamilton shaking me to life.

He finds me lying on the long seat of the caravan. To get to me, he had to step over the large obstacle of Ed Brennan, his father. It is still morning, and the first bad thought that comes to me is that it is cold: warm October is ending.

The second bad thought is that I am still alive, that I am not someone else, maybe this James Hamilton, leading a decent life into the future. And the third bad thought is gin, a drink I had not taken for some time, probably because of the gin hangover, the sense that it is still alive inside your brain, that it hasn't done with you yet.

I get to my feet and hit my head off the ceiling. My brain is still soaked in gin.

'I feel responsible,' James says. He is talking to me but looking at Ed, stretched out.

'Don't,' I say.

'I should have told you he was dead, or gone, or something.' He goes to the kitchen to boil the kettle for tea.

'We just talked about the old days . . . and drank . . . and drank,' I say.

'You've got less than a fortnight now.'

'I did up a little statement about my remorse and so forth.'

'Can I see it?'

'It's bullshit,' I say, handing it to him.

'That's all they're looking for,' he says.

As the kettle boils, he goes over to his father and kneels down. He looks at him, as though checking that he is still alive. 'He found you,' he says.

He still sounds unnecessarily guilty. But then I get a little rush of awareness from the gin, a jab of conscience telling me that some people have too much guilt – but then other people have too little.

'Cooney's,' I say.

I drink the tea, but it doesn't work the way tea usually does in the morning. It seems to set off a reaction with the gin, bringing it on again. Or maybe it's the realisation that this is a Sunday morning, and that James is still persevering with his terrible job, while his client slides into new levels of dissipation. James is taking out his papers and putting them on the table in front of us, but I am feeling so seedy I can hardly even summon up my normal levels of indifference. I am interested at this moment only in James himself, and in the big degenerate on the floor who is somehow his parent.

'Ah, shit.' I touch my cup off his, as a mark of solidarity.

'I'm sure the word is around the village now that you two were seen together . . .'

'Fuck them.'

'The sergeant will know.'

'Fuck him.'

'There's no harm having these guys onside.'

'Fuck him anyway.'

'It doesn't look great. Ideally you'd be at GA meetings in the church hall, not hanging around with the likes of . . . I feel responsible.'

Now the tea and the gin are giving me a little surge of elation. 'It's not you that should feel guilty, it's him – that he turned out the way he did, and you turned out the way you did,' I say.

'Thanks, Mr Devlin.'

'John.'

'Thanks, John. But I haven't turned out like anything yet. I'm only starting.'

'Whatever. At your age your father was already on his way down.'

We sit looking at the object of our discussion, lying there in a way that seems not too uncomfortable, as if he has grown accustomed to throwing himself down on any surface that becomes available. I consider telling James about Ed's great plans for me, how we should 'get back together', but in this setting it would compound the embarrassment.

'They say that the people who go to his place down there are the sort of people who couldn't get drink anywhere else,' James says.

'Sounds right.'

'I think he kinda enjoys the notoriety.'

'I know what you mean.'

'You enjoy it yourself?' he says, like he is interested in me, as a person.

'Nah. I'm thinking you used to have fellows around here who wanted everyone to think they were in the IRA. There was one particular clown who drove me across the border when I was about twelve, pointing to trees and telling me the British Army was hiding behind them . . . he wanted me, a child, to think he was notorious . . .'

'Ed wouldn't be making it up like that. Ed is kinda closer to the bad shit than that, from what I hear.'

'He was saying something about the good burghers, how they're in some sort of deep shit of their own?'

And then James makes another cup of tea and explains

to me a few things about those good burghers, and about the low-life of the area, and where Ed Brennan ranks in it these days.

He starts to talk about the Tallon case. He figures I must have heard about it, but I hadn't. It involves a prostitute called Mary Tallon, who was being used by a number of individuals around these parts, many of them respected members of the community, involved in business and law and local politics and good works. And when she turned sour for some reason, and started demanding money from a few of them, threatening to tell their wives, one of them killed her. He drove with her out to the forest where they usually did their thing, and somewhere out there he beat her to death. Probably with a spade. And he dug a hole and he buried her in it.

This guy, who is called Dinneen, and who is an electrician, is due to be charged with murder. And because he wasn't much good at it, he should be found guilty. But he figures he has nothing to lose by pleading not guilty anyway, and hoping for the best.

Which is causing the most horrible anxiety to various other worthies of the town, whose names appear in a notebook that Mary Tallon kept, which is now in the possession of her sister and of anyone with whom she wants to share it. James figures that Ed might be one of those people. Some of the men in the notebook have gone to Dinneen, trying to persuade him to plead guilty, to bury the matter. But he is determined not just to fight it all the way but to talk freely about all these other clients, if he feels it will help his defence. He will try to suggest that there are up to fifty men out there with a motive to murder Mary Tallon, and their names are all in the book.

'Ed's got the list?' I say.

'Probably . . . he knew the dead woman. She used to drink down there, in his place.'

'So, some of the finest men in this town really are in some shit?' I say, feeling a kind of a disgraceful satisfaction, which I hope James does not pick up.

'Let's go for a drive,' he says.

I leave the caravan door unlocked as I usually do, this time so that Ed can let himself out eventually. We get into James's car, a blue Mercedes that is about fifteen years old but a Mercedes all the same. It feels like James is physically removing me from my past, from my youth, from whatever I shared with Ed back then, and from the sickness of our reminiscences. James doesn't say where we're going, and I'm not sure if he actually knows.

We reach the top of the village and turn into the road where Philip Fraser used to live, in the old mansion he bought when one of his books became an international bestseller. I went in through those big black wrought-iron gates when I was delivering the post one Christmas, still the best job I ever had, I reckon, or the one I look back on most fondly. I didn't see Philip on any of the days when I delivered his cards and parcels, but each day I sneaked a look through the bay windows into that wonderful drawing room, which seemed to me like something out of a sumptuous BBC Sunday night costume drama. His housekeeper, a woman from the village, would take the post from me, and on the last day she gave me a five-pound note, from Mr and Mrs Fraser, which was exceptional.

Mr Fraser was an Englishman, one of those authors who came to live in Ireland to avoid paying tax. He used to cycle around the village in the summer wearing Bermuda shorts, which everyone thought was very strange. Early one Sunday morning I was looking out my bedroom window and I saw him walking down the promenade with someone who looked very like Sean Connery. I didn't really believe then that it could be Connery. I couldn't convince myself that he and I could inhabit the same place at the same time. Now I'm sure it was him, and I'm even sure they were discussing the making of a film version of one of Fraser's thrillers. I can see them sitting in the lovely floral-patterned armchairs in the drawing room, having a whiskey before dinner, which was made by Philip's wife, Minerva, the daughter of a Portuguese diplomat, a brilliant cook who would use produce grown in the gardens and in the greenhouse. In fact, Philip and Minerva were liked by the locals for the way they would give tomatoes from their greenhouse to various people who came to the house: the cleaner, the gardener, the girl who taught the piano to the children. And there was a lot of good feeling when Philip told some interviewer from the *Sunday Times* colour supplement that the village was now his home and that 'they're nice people'.

A couple of years later he moved to Portugal, where they also have nice people.

'You ever heard of Philip Fraser who lived in there? The author?' I say to James, as we pass the old house, which is now converted into apartments.

'No,' he says.

'Sean Connery?'

'Yes.'

'I saw him once, walking along the promenade.'

'Right.'

'He was working on a movie with Fraser, based on one of Fraser's books.'

'Right.'

James doesn't sound as impressed as I'd expected him to be. If anything, he sounds a small bit resentful. I keep talking, trying to remember. 'I could still tell you the name of every person who lived in each of these houses because I was a postman one Christmas. Not only could I tell you their names, I could tell you whether they gave me a tip or not. Best job I ever had, really good money, early start but finished by lunchtime. I remember cycling down this road on the big black bike with my hands off the handlebars, really looking forward to some gig the band was playing on

New Year's Eve. The band I managed, your father's band. For a few weeks there, I must have been happy.'

James swings the Mercedes in the direction of the town. 'Right,' he says.

'Then I'd take my wages to the betting office and I'd double them, treble them, maybe more. I started to call my wages "ammunition" ... I started to realise you didn't have to work ...'

'Shame you didn't lose, then,' he says.

'There was this old doggie man called Mickey Tuite, who took me to the greyhound track in the town a few times. I remember punting my wages and winning about two hundred quid on the Tote, sitting there counting it in the bar, waiting for the old man to finish his whiskey and drive me home ...'

'Right,' he grunts, apparently not impressed by this either.

We are well past the Fraser estate but he is still in my mind. 'I actually don't know for sure if Philip Fraser is still alive, but I think he probably is. Imagine him over there in Portugal, he must be ninety years of age now. That man who had made such a success of everything, who sat down with Sean Connery, is probably being wheeled around some other promenade, not knowing who he is or where he is.'

We are getting near the town now. James pulls into the car park of a row of shops – a mini-market, a dry cleaner's, a pizza place. For a few moments, he studies me. 'Are you still drunk?' he says.

'Probably.'

'I'm just trying to figure out how a man with less than two weeks left out here can be wasting his time remembering this shit that happened to you when you were seventeen, none of which will knock a month off your sentence. Do you actually realise that there's a difference between, say, seven years and four years?'

For the first time, he is sounding angry. Maybe finding his father on the floor brought it on. And it seems to come together for me, in this completely unexpected way, all the days I have spent up here in the present and in the past, all the distance I am keeping from my fate, now suddenly clarified.

'I don't think I'll be around for them to give me any sentence,' I say.

I have this strange sensation that I am hearing somebody else saying those words, while knowing that it is myself talking. And that there is truth in what I say, that I mean it. Except for one thing – if I really meant it, would I be saying it to someone else?

'Jesus,' James says, just a stunned little croak.

Maybe it is just the gin leaving me alone at last but I am overcome now by this feeling of abandonment, by how the world has turned against me, by the desolation of losing. I have had many other moments when not being around seemed like the solution but always I had some other thought to keep me going, some other way of looking at it, of connecting with the gambler's vast capacity for hope. But not on this occasion, not with this sharpened awareness of the future closing in on me, not when I have actually said it to someone else – yes, by saying to it someone else not only must I mean it but it is even starting to feel like a commitment. Maybe the only one that I am going to honour.

'Sorry,' I say.

James Hamilton shifts in the driver's seat as if he's trying to get a fuller view of me, to assess the true nature of my condition. 'Do you mean you'll try to leave the country?'

I am going to try to leave the world, I think, but I don't give voice to that. I just marvel that even in this situation a smart answer came into my head. 'No, James. That's not what I mean.'

'I was getting angry with you. Sorry,' he says.

'Fuck that, James.'

'I wasn't trying to freak you out. I was trying to get you to focus.'

'I'm not going to be in that courtroom.'

'I'll get some coffee.'

He goes to buy some in the mini-market, as if that will make a difference. He leaves me in the car alone, which vaguely disappoints me, as if he doesn't really believe I am a danger to myself.

By the time he returns with two containers of coffee I have decided that the way to do this is to walk out into the sea.

CHAPTER 8

He thought that bringing me to this grim little shopping centre would make me feel better. Not because of the coffee, which is bad, but because while we drink it, we can look at the man who sold it to us, the owner of the mini-market, Brian Gill.

'I hear he's on the list. I hear that Mary was touching him for money above and beyond,' James says.

We go quiet for a while, looking at this Brian Gill serving behind the counter of his shop, just some thin guy, with black hair going grey, in a V-necked golf jumper and respectable trousers, who is getting through the day, selling the Sunday papers, nothing in his demeanour to tell you that he is suffering, that he got unlucky. That he is a brother of mine.

I know that, most of the day, he is carrying this lump of anxiety around inside him, that it rises and falls and rises again with the constancy of a vital organ, this thing we call a sick heart. And that there are times when he is released from it by some mechanism of the mind, some signal that stops it overloading, that even makes him forget about it for an hour here and there, but that always switches it back on late at night, when he can think of nothing else, except this: he is on the wrong side of the line.

And what did he do? He paid someone to have sex with him, like a lot of other guys who run a lot of other stores in a lot of other towns, and who can walk around with a light heart because they got the kind of regular, everyday breaks you need to stay on the right side of the line, the breaks that were somehow denied to him. Yes, that is how he narrates it to himself with the part of him that remains rational, like a sad saxophone taking the lead for a few moments, until all the old noise returns to torment him.

Still we sit here in the Mercedes looking at him serving customers, and he is brisk and cheerful and even having a laugh. It's like that brief impression of people you get when you're on a train and you're passing their houses and you see them in there, these slightly mysterious figures disconnected from all their worries.

'You know him?' I say.

'Good guy.'

'Good guy?'

'Raises money for the Children of Chernobyl and that sort of thing.'

'Does his wife know?'

'No idea.'

I figure it might even be more difficult for him to tell his wife than it was for me to tell Christina, given the nature of his offence. I probably came close a few times to telling Christina, letting her know that I was having a bad run, but even when I was crucified with fear at four in the morning, always, always I believed in my own power to make it all right. Maybe, in the deepest part of me, I still do.

Maybe Brian Gill here is doing the same thing, hoping to get out on the last race.

'Who knows about the list?' I say.

'Most of the town by now. But they don't know exactly who's on it. I know five or six names, from talking to guards and to other lawyers. In fact one of them's a guard.'

'And you thought it would make me feel better to come here and have a look at one of them?'

'He didn't kill her but, still, if his name comes out . . . you wouldn't want to be that guy, would you?' he says.

'Maybe not . . . but I still wouldn't want to be myself.'

'At least your problems are out in the open.'

'You're right about that too.'

He crushes the paper coffee cup into a ball. He gives me

that look again, studying me. When he speaks, he sounds composed in the way that borders on the legalistic. It's like he needs to compose himself because, to his credit, the job doesn't come naturally to him.

'A few minutes ago, you gave me the distinct impression that you were suicidal . . .' he says.

I grunt in acknowledgement.

'If you'll forgive me saying so, that's good,' he says.

'You mean, in terms of the bullshit?'

'In terms of showing signs of remorse. Of being able to furnish the court with—'

'But I won't be there.'

He looks away, trying to work it out. 'OK . . . let's say you . . . you think better of it.'

'OK . . . let's pretend.'

'We can have a professional opinion that you've been deep in addiction, even to the point of being suicidal, and that you're now attending meetings.'

'And that means I get maybe four years. Sorry, my way is better.'

James goes quiet for a moment, as if I have defeated him. 'Maybe my father's pushed you into this. Did he say something to you?'

'He said nothing to me that I didn't know already. He even said some things that were right, and true.'

James gives me a look that says he doesn't like the sound of that. 'You need something to eat,' he says.

As he swings the Mercedes out onto the main road into the town, he starts questioning me about my diet, as if this, too, might knock a few months off my time in the slammer. As if he's chosen to ignore what I have just said to him, that I won't be doing any time anywhere. When I describe my diet to him, he figures that living on fish and chips and Coke may be both a symptom and a further cause of my depression.

But I don't want to eat, not in a restaurant, not now. I ask him to take me back to the caravan, where at least I can be myself, where I don't run the risk of being refused a table by some restaurant manager, or of causing offence by insisting that there be no coleslaw. I am still mesmerised by my own thoughts of walking into the sea, mesmerised, too, that I'd never seriously considered it before, as if it took a night on the booze with Ed to move me the extra inch that was needed. Ah, is it just the gin? Is it just that?

No, it's everything, every damn thing that has happened in my life up until this point, with just one extra thing – just time. I have run out of time.

When we get back to the caravan the normal thing would be for James to drop me there and to drive off, but it's different now. I have a great need to be on my own, to cut myself off from everything, yet I also have this need to talk, like I need to explain myself to James, to justify this thing I have landed on him.

And now he's carrying an even greater burden of care,

because in addition to minimising the millions of euro worth of harm I have done, he probably feels he needs to keep an eye on me. Up to a point, at least, that point being completely unknown to either of us.

So we are doing this nervous dance, sitting in the car just trying to work out the form that the rest of the day will take.

'You think my father's still in there?' he says.

'Do you want him to be?'

'Not really.'

'I'd say he's gone.'

'Or he could have just frozen to death.'

On this first day of November, with the temperature gauge on the dashboard telling us it is minus one degree, that does not sound too fanciful. It's enough to get us from the car to the caravan, to see that Ed has gone. I guess the alcoholic, even in a sort of coma, will always find a way to avoid an awkward engagement on the morning after.

'I'll stay with you for a while . . . if that's OK,' James says.

I have this urge to prostrate myself in front of him with gratitude, and another urge to tell him to go away and let me be.

'You must have other clients . . . other assholes?' I say.

'I've cleared my diary.'

'Even if you move in here with me you won't be able to stop me.'

'I know that. But I don't think you're going to do it.'

I get the Super Ser going. The two of us hunker down in front of it, rubbing our freezing hands.

'You mean, I could never leave all this behind?'

James gets up and goes to the kitchen. He makes tea. 'If you were really serious about it, I don't think you'd have told me,' he says.

'I didn't mean to. It just came out of me.'

I am only myself starting to understand the nature of this, the way that thoughts of suicide can be a comfort to a down-going man. I am feeling that comfort now because it does away with something more terrifying, the fact that in this situation I am powerless. That the very best I can do for myself is to offer myself up to the mercy of people who are not much better than I am, just a bit luckier. And when I get past this powerlessness of the man pleading guilty to all charges, and I think of the powerlessness of being in jail, it is worse than any notion of oblivion.

Now I have this sense that there is something I can do, that they can't stop me doing. Maybe it's the gambler in me, deciding that if I am going to be the game for these people, I would like a piece of the action. So I'd be playing God, which has a kind of consistency to it, because it was playing God that got me here, making my money by predicting the future, arrogant enough to try to ordain my own fate. I am even seeing a vision of the deed itself, which has a kind of a wistful beauty, with me walking out for maybe half a mile to meet the incoming tide, and just standing there as it washes over me, looking back at the village and imagining the place as it used to be, and how good it was, so that the last thing I see as the water takes me down is the amusements in the summer.

I am only wondering now why I didn't think of this before.

Then James calls me to the kitchen. He is studying the screen of the laptop, which is displaying the website of an online gambling firm, in particular the account of Ed Brennan. There is two thousand euro in the account.

So Ed didn't just come up here to berate me for my character defects, to writhe around for a while in the bittersweet mess of our adolescence. It was not all just gin-talk: he is really offering me some of his own money to bet with, an act of real kindness if you leave out the fact that I am probably the best-known compulsive gambler in the country and that this would start me up again. Already it is sending a lovely wave of adrenalin through me.

Oh, Ed, I think. Oh, Ed, you are a twisted and a terrible man. But still I can see that, in your way, you are trying to help me here. In these days of darkness you are showing me some great prospect, some crooked way out of this. Or maybe you are just causing trouble. Maybe that's all you're doing.

'Let's get out,' James says, marching me towards the car.

CHAPTER 9

I tell James about it on the way to the restaurant, the suggestion by Ed that if about a hundred things went right for me with the gambling, and not one thing went wrong, I might be able to pay some meaningful amount back to my two main accusers, which might persuade the judge to go easy on me.

I would like to tell him about Annie, and about the letters I wrote to her, and about the feeling that came over me when Ed brought it all back up, but I have already felt his rebuke for such wanderings.

And, anyway, at this moment I am beyond that feeling. I have this other energy that came to me when we found the money in the account, a dangerous energy, which James picked up from me, getting me out of there to a place where we can eat and talk like civilised men. I find that I really want to go there now, and I am getting impatient because the restaurant he has chosen is a few miles on the other side of the town. I want to eat, which implies to me that maybe I want to live. For a few more hours at least, a few more days.

I am talking too much, thinking too fast. I am helpless again.

We will have steak, James and I, in this candle-lit restaurant with nobody else in it. The black tables and chairs and the general darkness of the atmosphere bring me back to that couple in the village who were having an affair and were ostracised. Except this place is empty just because it's a Sunday afternoon and because there's not much money in the town anymore, not much in the country, after all of us fearless punters had done with it.

James orders a couple of whiskeys – a proper drink – and while I'm still high on life's possibilities, he puts a little Dictaphone in front of me, to get me to talk about my punting, just mine, with no added commentary on the crisis of capitalism in general, how it had become a global Ponzi scheme in which players such as myself were the little guys. He wants none of that shit, just a description of how I did it and who I did it to and how it felt, so he can show something to the barrister who will take over from him in court, who can use it as evidence of my unflinching honesty in facing up to my disgraceful acts.

Yes, I think he may be a decent fellow, James, who may even be pretty good at his job. He has accepted that he's not going to get anything else in writing from me, anything that is any good, that I just don't have the heart for it, that I am worn out and that it's too late now. But he hasn't given up, and now he is taking his chance, putting this machine in front of me while the humour is on me. That is smart, and sensitive, and it shows tenacity, too, after a day in which I have shown myself to be, at the very least, unstable – and maybe I will show myself to be worse again, at some point in the few hours to come, a few hours to midnight and then another day of the few that will remain.

If I wasn't so wasted I might have been able to appreciate that there is something riding on this for James too, that he could make a name for himself as the man who got me a light sentence, an achievement that would ensure every other major asshole in the country will come looking for him to do the same trick for them.

And what do I owe him for bringing him the sight of his father lying like a tramp on the floor of the caravan? I guess that when you're in the law business, as James is, dealing with difficult and dangerous people, such scenes of dissipation would not be entirely strange.

Nor does he seem offended that Ed is still trying to dream up ways to help me out without needing to use the services of my lawyer. If any disrespect was intended, James hasn't bothered to pick it up. I rate him for that, too, for not being petty about it.

'Adrenalin . . . adrenalin is what this is about,' I say.

James just nods and sips his whiskey. He checks that the Dictaphone is running.

Yes, adrenalin. I can feel it at this moment, all wrong now, in spirit, and probably all in vain, but still adrenalin, the substance on which I lived for a long time. I heard this old warrior at a racecourse once, saying that adrenalin is great stuff if you can get your hands on it. But the thing about it is, you don't have to go looking for it anywhere: they've never been able to make anything as good as the stuff that's already inside you, waiting to be activated.

Which isn't going to happen by walking in the woods or by learning how to cook or by any of those activities that are described as therapeutic but which, to be honest, will never really make you feel as fulfilled as you do when you make an enormous load of money without working. That is what makes you rounded. That is what makes you whole.

James, can I tell you how I felt when I was doing a law degree in UCD – or, rather, not doing a law degree in UCD – and I won so much money playing poker around town I was able to buy a little terraced house in the Coombe? Can I describe to you the feeling of fulfilment I used to get when I woke up every morning and I looked around my little bedroom and I remembered that I had won this? I had not earned it, or inherited it, or robbed it . . . I had won it.

Can I convey to you, James, the pleasure I felt in the knowledge I was that good at something? And that it was something which didn't involve getting up out of bed in the morning to go into some horrible office full of solicitors – sorry, James, it is not for me – or having much daily contact of any kind with this thing they call reality? When I was around your age, James, I discovered that I was good and that, as result, I was free.

It was better than that: I was good at something that most people are very bad at, which made me a member of an elite, even subversive, force, going against a gambling business that is basically involved in the creation of bad gamblers on a fantastic scale.

In fact, better still, poker turned out to be the lesser of my talents, a little behind betting on sports, which is where most of the really bad gamblers are to be found. And, like a sportsman, my ability lay in being able to strike this strange balance between being fiercely engaged, and not really giving a damn.

To be good, you have to give it your best, but you also have to have the gift of not caring, to help you to deal with your darkest enemy, which is the pain of losing. The good gambler will feel this pain far more acutely than the bad gambler, who tends to think more about winning, about the glory of backing the winner of the Grand National at a big price, that romantic stuff.

I guess they know in their souls that they are bad, so

they don't have as much riding on it as the good ones, and often they don't even count their losses. They think only of the happy days, because it is not as important for them as it is for us, so proud of our ability to stay on the right side of that line.

So we fear losing, because we are proud, and losing tears the heart out of us, making us feel worthless. Which explains why I always had this kind of Hippocratic oath, which said, 'First, do not lose.' And if you must lose try to develop that most precious of instincts which will enable you to lose small.

And that is why a true professional gambler will tend to bet rarely, and will keep it simple – unless he virtually knows the result in advance, he will not indulge. The fear of losing is too great, greater even than that described by certain sportsmen, who at least could play an active part in getting the right result.

The gambler, after he puts the money down, is powerless to intervene. So he has to be sure of his own rightness. He has to be convinced that he is going to walk away from every engagement with more than he had when he started, because any other thought is unbearable.

And yet, somehow, in the depths of this unmerciful dread, he also needs to be indifferent, to have a quiet mind, to be able to make enormous decisions as if they have no consequence of any kind. And that is the gift.

And, James, I had it.

James orders another whiskey for me and another for himself. The waiter brings the drinks with no difficulty, as if he has no idea who I am, as if it doesn't matter that we are both beyond the legal limit for driving, in this restaurant three miles outside the town. Then he brings the steaks, as if they will soak it up.

'You call it a gift. Is it not also a disease?' James says, not quite swept away by my enthusiasm for my old profession.

'It is only a disease if you lose,' I say.

'Right.'

'I'm not trying to be smart here, James. It's true. If you're a few million ahead nobody talks about you having a disease. They'd put your picture on the front page of the paper if they could, toasting your success. It is only the losers who have the disease.'

'But everybody loses. I mean, in the end.'

'Not everybody,' I say.

'But as close as makes no difference?'

'Even if it's only one that wins, James, even if it's only one . . .'

I have not been eating much steak of late, and I try not to wolf it all down, just for appearances. I hope that James is paying. I take him back again, to my little house in the Coombe that I bought – no, that I won – for fifty grand long before the thing took hold.

'All the way through the thing I kept that house. Nobody else ever came into it,' I say.

'Christina?'

'She thought it was some kind of an office I kept in the city. She had no interest.'

'And you didn't tell her?'

'I never spoke about my gambling.'

'But she knew the house had a sentimental value?'

'She wasn't one for looking back.'

James seems a bit lost there, maybe thinking of some situation in his own life, maybe the whiskey confusing him a bit. So I try to clarify.

'Christina and I didn't have much sentiment in our relationship, not a lot of what you might call feelings. What we had was money. And money is a beautiful thing, especially when it comes to you by magic. It is so beautiful. It has such an energy of its own – it can get a lot of people through their entire lives without an angry word.'

'You don't really believe that?' he says.

'Even if you've never read a book, even if you don't have much of a mind or even a soul, money can make you seem like a serious person. A grand old house that you own completely, with four cars parked outside it, worth about a million all told, can make you feel you're living right. And Christina was actually born into money, so she never really had to try too hard – there were a lot of things she never had to see, never had to know.'

James is agitated now. 'You talk about her as if she was just one of those women in the gossip columns, the lunches for charity . . .'

'Well, that's what she was, James.'

'So what did you have in common?'

'Money. One more time, money. Money is the word, James, and money is the man. I guess I was interesting for her, because there was a bit of mystery around me and the way I made money. And I had excellent manners, and I was tall and good-looking, and she was tall and good-looking, and we connected well in bed. And then there was the money.'

'OK,' he says, enough with the money.

'I kinda drifted into it, maybe thinking I should be getting married to someone, thinking I should be doing something normal. It was a great weakness in me, an aberration, thinking that this was the mature thing to do, that I couldn't just keep on living the way I was living, like some character from the Old West, a sporting man. Thinking that a regular marriage and an orderly existence would round everything off, when really it was just some fear that was eating at me, the guilt we all have, even those of us who have known freedom. Ah, it kills me now to think of what a fool I was to compromise, to forget for a while how beautiful that freedom had been, how hard I had earned it, only to lose it . . . ah, I hate losing, I hate it so much.'

'In my opinion, Christina's a stunningly attractive woman. That's just me,' he says.

'I can see that . . . I can still see that, despite it all. And probably with most other men she would have had a good life. We were great for about six months, and then we got to know one another and it wasn't so great. Then she just wanted me to be somebody else, and I wanted her to be somebody else. I blame myself, truly, for wandering into her world so foolishly, into a place in which I just did not belong. But I was still surprised at how hard she was in the end, how unforgiving.'

'Maybe you shouldn't be surprised. I mean, some of the people whose money you lost were friends of hers. She introduced them to you. How could she not be angry?'

'But no one was blaming her. They were blaming me.'

'You're blaming her. You blame her for spending so much money, you blame her for the way she reacted when she heard.'

'OK, you're right. And I hate that in myself. I hate the fact that it makes me a loser all over again, this bitterness.'

'Maybe if you spoke to her one more time before the court case, just to apologise or whatever.'

'You think I didn't apologise?'

'OK.'

'Fuck's sake, James. I kinda knew I had done wrong here.'

'Maybe she'd feel different about it now, with you probably going to jail and that.'

'No, I don't think so. Until you become a rich solicitor you'll never understand the way those people live. They have no souls, I'm telling you, they have no souls. You know the way that people like me and your father used to spend a lot of our time and energy on stuff like music and books and films and so forth? On what you might call the life of the mind? Those people don't have minds. At least, they don't have minds in the sense that I'm talking about. They don't use their minds for any purpose but the making and the keeping and the spending and the accumulating of money. They really have no idea why anyone would listen to a JJ Cale album and have an opinion about it, because there is but one thought in their heads – how much did it sell? They're not putting that on, they're not striking an attitude, it's just that they do not have those parts of the brain some of us have, which we use in these wasteful pursuits. They have something there, but it's made of different stuff, a kind of pure aggression that drives the constant pursuit of money, and more money. They are able to marshal all their energies for the one purpose. If they wish to have some involvement in the arts, they will buy it. Or they will buy someone who will do it for them. That is their world. And for some reason, for a while, I was attracted to that. It turned me on.'

James points his whiskey glass at me. He isn't eating much of his steak. I think he is a bit drunk. 'I happen to know that you made some very large donations to good causes – the homeless,' he says.

Yes he does sound a bit drunk. 'The guilt again, that we all have.'

'Fifty grand a year during the good times?'

'A lot of guilt.'

'I want to use that in court.'

'Where did you hear it?'

'You know a lot of rich people? Well, I know a lot of poor people,' he says, with a hint of whiskey-flavoured pride that he's nailed it there.

'You can't use it in court. I will deny it.'

'So you'll lie on oath, too?'

'I gave that money without wishing to be named, for the good of my soul, and to claim it now would be so completely lacking in class, I couldn't do it.'

James slumps back in an exasperated, definitely half-drunk state. 'You know what I think?' he says.

'What?' I say, because he wants me to.

'You've told me a few times now that you're a good gambler. I think you're actually a bad gambler . . . a bad gambler. And maybe a good man.'

'You've been drinking, James.'

'I'll tell you why you're a bad gambler. Because all gamblers are bad gamblers. You guys don't seem to get that bit. No matter how "good" you are.'

He makes me laugh with his air quotes around the 'good'. Old-fashioned, it seems.

'OK, James. This is the sort of gambler I am,' I say.

James checks that his machine is still working. He signals for another couple of whiskeys, and I tell him about the specific charge of the half a million I took from a man called Thomas Gaskin. I tell him about the thing going down, and about the money system going wrong for guys like me, about the end of our world.

A few months earlier Thomas Gaskin, a chap I knew well from college, a kind of a gentleman farmer in Wicklow, sold some land and made half a million. He could have just stuck his cash in the post office or buried it in a black plastic sack on his lovely farm in Wicklow but he gave it to me, because he wanted just a little bit more. They all wanted just that little bit more.

And I needed them, too, despite my nonchalance. Towards the end I needed a Thomas Gaskin every few weeks, when the others came looking for the return on their investment, as they called it, when I couldn't stall them in my charming way with talk of reinvestment in a new shopping centre in Berlin or an apartment block in Miami. And, yes, many of these places actually existed: I was not some fantasist running your basic pyramid scheme. I bought buildings and I sold them and I had documents to prove it, and I had actual profits to distribute. It was just that I never had quite enough.

I needed to be backing a few winners too, to make the nut.

So when the thing started going down, I knew I was going to be getting more visitors than usual to the grand old house, and that they would be looking for their money, all of it, right now, no excuses. So I spent a lot of time in my little house in the Coombe, trying to hold back the avalanche, mainly by punting Thomas Gaskin's money and that of another man on the official rap sheet, a guy called William Finn who, in the fat years, used to own a piece of some small town in the west and had given me his last three hundred grand just a few weeks before Gaskin. The last in, they were, maybe, the unluckiest, and though they could never, ever acknowledge it, for reasons that I accept, I did my best for them. As I did for them all.

I needed to turn that half-million and that three hundred grand into about eight million, very, very quickly. I had fifteen laptops in the living room, working my accounts with all the online betting operators in the universe, who were happy enough to take the large amounts I was staking, because at the end of every day, somehow, when I worked it all out, I was losing. I was losing and I could not stop losing and I knew why I was losing but I knew, too, that I couldn't possibly stop.

I was losing because I just didn't have the time it takes to win, or the calmness, or the detachment, or the discretion. I just had this desperate urgency and this overwhelming fear, sitting there shattered most nights with nothing to divert me but the latest load of emails from equally desperate men, or their solicitors or their accountants, demanding to see me and to get their money back. And then, as the man said, even after losing so much, you find out you can always lose a little more.

But I could feel it coming for a while. For maybe six months it had been getting away from me. I had been losing in ways I had never lost before, really horrible reverses that should have told me I was doomed. I have a particularly brutal recollection of one of these blows because I feel it demonstrates more than any of the others, that the baleful gods were coming after me. I had backed Arsenal to beat Newcastle away, a bet I utterly believed in, a bet I desperately needed to win. So I had 250 grand on that, at about evens, not just because I fancied it but because I really needed to be punting such amounts in order to fill the hole. It took me half the day getting that money on with various online bookies, in bets of ten grand or twenty grand. But I got it on, and soon it was clear that I had called it right. The Arsenal were 3–0 up after ten minutes, celebrating with almost every kick of the ball, and back in the Coombe I celebrated with them. They were 4–0 up at half-time. I was already making decisions about how I was going to reinvest the quarter-of-a-million that was most certainly coming to me. And then Abou Diaby of Arsenal was sent off early in the second half. And then Newcastle scored. But still I was not getting nervous, partly because it hardly ever happens in professional football that a team has been leading by four goals and does not win. And then Newcastle scored again. Now I was getting nervous, getting jumpy, but the better part of me was still complimenting myself on winning the bet. I was seeing this little revival of Newcastle's as their contribution to what we call 'garbage time', an American term denoting that period in a game when the result is already obvious, the battle has been won and lost, but there's still a fair few minutes to be played. Sometimes a team lacking in character will put on a bit of a display in garbage time, without ever really threatening to get a result. And Newcastle in particular would be such a team, I was thinking, and then they scored a third goal. Now I could feel the sickness starting inside me, not just a sickness of the spirit but an urge to vomit, like a kid who's just got horribly drunk for the first time, a sense that everyone associated with Arsenal on this day, including those of us who had 250 grand on them, was connected to some misfortune bigger than ourselves.

Newcastle, all heroes now, scored a magnificent fourth goal, you knew it was coming. The match ended in a 4–4 draw.

I remember another match I lost around that time, in similarly hideous circumstances, after which the defeated coach, who was from somewhere in the Balkans, said that he would be haunted by it forever; they all would. And when you heard the way he said it, his heavy-hearted Balkan sincerity, you knew he wasn't just putting out a line, but that they really would be haunted by it forever.

And if you think that in the months that followed I had a few more situations like that, which will haunt me forever, James, you can start to understand the shape I'm in.

CHAPTER 10

The whiskey is making James talk about feelings. He wants to know how I felt when I finally told Christina, how I felt when I told Thomas Gaskin and William Finn when they came to the house. And how I felt in the solicitor's office when I sat there as the solicitor explained to four other people that I had lost their money and that there was absolutely no chance of them ever getting it back.

I tell him that Christina took it the worst in the sense that she physically attacked me. Thomas Gaskin took it the best, seeming to hate himself as much as he hated me. The others were somewhere in between, I can't rightly recall because by that time I was destroyed.

I had to tell Christina because Gaskin was already leaving Wicklow, on his way to our house to confront me. He had been sending emails and texts compulsively, and finally that morning, I texted him back. Just *OK*. That was my moment of defeat. That's how it seems to happen for me, without much preparation, not much rehearsal, just *OK*. It's like I'm in the Alamo, and I don't stop shooting, or I can't stop shooting, until the moment that it's just not possible to keep doing that anymore. Then I surrender and everything is different.

So when I texted Thomas Gaskin it was also a message to myself, that the gambling had to stop now. Maybe that moment could not have come any other way. Maybe if I'd imagined it many times, I would have found it so terrifying I could never actually have pressed the button: *OK*.

I had got up and got dressed and had coffee with Christina, as if it was going to be just another day working the screens in the Coombe, another burst of betting action in this everlasting now. I was even getting to tolerate the self-loathing that I would feel each morning as I listened to her organising her days of tennis and lunch, unaware that a shit-rain was coming, and that the rest of her life was going to be about picking up the wreckage.

She knew that the thing had gone wrong, even for people like us, but I don't think it occurred to her in any meaningful way that we were about to go down the way we did. She had never thought of us as being anything other than successful, a smashing couple. She would actually call us a smashing couple, as people usually do when they're talking about some other couple, as if she was constantly checking that we were doing all the things we should be doing, whatever was right for people like us. That was her job.

I believe she was very good at it, too, that she had taste and she had style, and that she had some sincere interest in raising money for worthy causes. Her family had had money for long enough to feel they could relax about their own situation and get into the charity game. And while her two brothers were bad lads, happiest doing nothing, letting others run the business while they ponced around, Christina took up that obligation. She was, it must be said, the best of them. She once set up an auction that raised a load of money for the homeless, a really worthy cause in my view, even before it became personally relevant to me. But even the bullshit causes got her full attention, bullshit here being defined as something to do with a country that is not your own – Kosovo or Sudan – and the further away the country, the greater the bullshit. I would even say to her, and she would not dismiss it, that anyone who can't find enough misfortune in their own land is not looking hard enough.

But I would never run her down because I knew how much she put into it. I guess her friends assumed she was doing it as a reaction to some emptiness in her life because we didn't have children, but we never spoke about that even as a possible reason. I believe she would have been doing it anyway, and that I would have been doing what I was doing, regardless of whom I was married to, whether I had children or not. It worked well for me, to have this endless need to be magicking up large amounts of money. Because while Christina wanted a better life for the world's poor, she didn't feel there was anything to be gained by becoming one of them.

And that job of staying rich was to be taken care of on my side of the house. It even gave me an edge as a gambler to know that she was depending on me, that all of our beautiful things were depending on me, that this island in the kitchen, built for eighty grand, at which we had our coffee every morning, was depending on me, that this great house was depending on me. Hell, even those less fortunate than ourselves were depending on me. I wasn't just one of those fellows who go to Vegas wearing a big floppy green hat, calling himself a high-roller. No, I wasn't one of those characters. I am bored by them and their fantasies about being Amarillo Slim or the Cincinnati Kid. I was better than them and I was surrounded by all the evidence of that.

The only luxury I didn't have was the luxury of losing, and I think that gave me an edge. To know that I could not lose, and that if I did somehow, I could not lose again for a long time after that. I just could not do that – or the world, and everything in it, would end.

Which it did, on that morning, not with Armageddon but with a little 'bloop', the sound of a text being sent: *OK*.

A few seconds before I sent it, I was talking to Christina about maybe selling my old Triumph sports car and maybe not buying anything to replace it, and things were peaceful between us. And a few seconds after it she was physically attacking me, beating the shit out of me, and she couldn't stop, and I couldn't stop her, and maybe I didn't want to stop her.

In the few seconds before, as I finished my coffee and the text from Gaskin came through, I tried to slide off my high stool as usual, and make it to the front door, but I couldn't. I just could not face another day of gambling, another day of losing. I had so little gambling money left that even I had run out of hope. And the money that was not for gambling did not exist anymore.

In those last moments I had before the revelation, I became fixated on the marble counter of the island at which I was sitting, contemplating how poignant it seemed now, remembering all that I had won, all the right calls I had made, just for this lump of stone. Remembering that I'd lived for a long time in a house I was ashamed to bring anyone into, that I had come so far from that place to get to here.

'Everything is gone,' I said.

She put her cup of coffee on the counter, with undue care, as if afraid she would let it fall. I could not read her reaction: her face seemed inanimate – her spirit seemed to be absent.

I carried on talking. 'I've lost everything we have, and I've lost everything belonging to our friends. I'm sorry . . . I'm so sorry. I thought I could keep it all going but I can't do it anymore . . . They'll call it a Ponzi scheme . . . I'll probably go to jail . . . I'm sorry.'

When the words were out of me, each line spoken quietly and clearly and then a little pause and then the next line, and then the word 'jail', they seemed to drag everything else out of me too, and I felt this urge to vomit. I ran to the sink, and while I was bent over it puking, Christina was working out her own trauma by tearing at my hair and banging my head against the tap. There was no theatrical delay between the delivery of the information and the moment it started sinking in. There was no discussion or dispute. I guess she must have known by the state of me that there was no other way of looking at this except to realise straight away that it was true, and to go fucking crazy.

I could not resist her in any way. I loathed myself so much in those days that her reaction seemed just about right. She dragged me to the floor and she kicked me a few times, full force to the body. Instinctively I tried to protect myself but I didn't try to get away from her. I thought of that line in the Bible about the man who gains the whole world but suffers the loss of his soul, and now I know what happens to the man who loses the whole world. He is just a despicable heap of bones to be kicked around, a disgusting creature who was given so many of the talents of a human being and was not grateful but instead went back to the gods looking for more, and more, in this most egotistical way. And who was given more, and more, but was still not grateful, only drunk, drunk with pride.

I can remember just one other thought that I had in those moments of rage and hatred, the observation that as she was kicking me she was wearing tennis shoes. When she stopped she, too, seemed exhausted. She was breathless and letting out little shrieks, like an athlete just after an especially brutal session in the gym. I said something but I got no answer. She was on her way to the door and out to the car, as if she might catch some awful sickness if she stayed any longer with me. I don't know where she went, but I don't think she was going to play tennis.

James should definitely be drunk now, but he seems to be listening carefully, maybe even looking for entertainment. A few salient facts, too, but also entertainment. Everyone loves a loser's tale.

He's talking about driving home, and that is fine by me. A bit of drunk driving will set me off on another little journey into the land of my youth, and it will be liberating – if he drives into a tree, and I am killed, that is also fine by me.

Nor does the waiter make any comment as James pays the bill and we leave the restaurant and walk with all that booze on board towards the car park. All afternoon and through the evening, serving me without giving the slightest sign of disapproval, and now letting us drive home full of whiskey, he seems determined not to be a pain in the arse. It is so strange to me now to encounter such plain kindness in this unkind country.

But it is very cold tonight, and it is very dark, one of those nights you might look up at the moon to see if it still exists. I don't need the moon to remind me that I haven't got much time left out here, but I look up anyway. Even this unlovely night now sends a little ache of regret through me, these aches that are starting to become more frequent as the time runs down.

We sit in the car with the engine running, to get the heat going. He hands me the Dictaphone, in case I feel like sharing a bit more of my ruination. There's a journey of about six miles ahead of us, three miles into the town and then three miles out to the village, which is a lot for a driver who is well over the limit. Even one who would know a lot of the guards around these parts.

'I know we should get a taxi . . . but now that you've started I don't want you to stop,' he says, with some clarity for a man who should be intoxicated.

He eases the old Mercedes out of the restaurant car park and onto a country road. He drives slowly, but not quite so slowly that it would obviously betray his night's drinking. I get the feeling he has done this before.

I give him a bit more talk for his Dictaphone, to keep us both awake . . .

I was on the kitchen floor still, maybe for half an hour I was lying there, feeling that this was a natural state for me to be in, a fitting conclusion. Or maybe it was some primal force bearing down on me, leaving me in the foetal position, longing to return to the beginning but knowing that this was the end of everything.

She hadn't kicked me in the head, but she'd caused some damage by banging it against the tap. I could feel a raw wound just over the ear and figured it was bleeding. They were well-made taps.

I could also smell vomit, which had clung to the shoulder of my jacket, along with the vomit that had stayed in the sink. Mostly it was my arms and legs that hurt, but as I eventually unwound myself, it seemed that I could stand up and walk to the bathroom to have a look at my face. Thomas Gaskin, after all, was on his way to meet me. I would need to arrange myself, to freshen up. Then I would need a few cups of coffee, a few brandies.

Christina wouldn't have wanted it, but I reckon it was her violence that saved me. I don't exactly know why Gaskin didn't do some terrible harm to me, but I guess it was something to do with the going-over I had had already. The wound over my ear had started to bleed again as I opened the door to him. The air of sickness and destruction that I carried with me as I brought him through the hall may have taken the edge off his anger. But I think he was also preoccupied with his own failure, his own greed. He was a careful, pleasant and neatly proportioned man in a suit and a shirt and a tie, who would have been completely unsuited to the farming life, even the gentlemanly version in which he had dabbled. And though he enjoyed all the cash that came to him from the sale of the land, he'd had no great notions of becoming a player, until the day he met me in the barber shop of the Shelbourne Hotel, and we got talking. Somehow, a few hours later in the bar upstairs, he found himself departing from all that he knew and engaging in the biggest transaction of his life. For that one mistake, that most unlucky encounter, he had been hammered into the dirt.

Now, as he sat in my kitchen, on the same high stool on which Christina had been sitting, I gave him roughly the same few shattering lines I had given to her. But he didn't seem to have the energy to launch an assault on me. He was just appallingly quiet.

He didn't drink the brandy I had left on the marble counter for him, in the glass that he would not accept from my hand. He just kept whispering, 'Fuck, fuck, fuck,' staring into some distant dimension where all of life's badness is to be found, no doubt wondering how he was going to say this to the woman he had married six months ago in Wicklow, with a reception in a marquee in the grounds of her father's great house. In this he was a bit like me, a guy who had made a few quid and married into a family with serious money. And knowing that sort of person as I do, I figured Gaskin was going to get slapped around for a while, for calling it so wrong. So he just kept staring into that distant dimension, whispering, 'Fuck, fuck, fuck.'

He had known me when we were younger, pretending to be students. He had probably formed an opinion of me back then as a decent enough sort, and he couldn't quite work out if this made the betrayal all the greater, or if the two of us were just cursed by whatever weaknesses of character had drawn us to one another in the first place. And even at that, everything would have been all right if he had not decided to go to the barber that day.

James pulls into the side of the road, maybe a mile outside the town. He parks smoothly, even soberly, as if my narrative has sharpened his concentration. But, then, he is young, so young.

'There's a case to be made that your life has been totally destroyed already. You have already suffered so much that a long jail sentence would be plainly unjust,' he says.

'The way I look at it, if we even mention any suffering on my part they'll throw another five years at me,' I say.

'You have had violence done to you. Grievous bodily harm.'

'I'd really prefer if you didn't use that.'

'So you don't want us to mention . . .'

'It's not just her dignity, it's mine too.'

'You don't want us to mention that. You don't want us to mention the large amounts you gave to charity either. You won't even drop in to a meeting of Gamblers Anonymous just to pass the time—'

'I'll go to a meeting,' I interrupt.

James loses his bearings for a moment. Maybe I, too, have lost my bearings but I can't keep saying no to him, saying no to myself. I have lost even the energy for that.

And though I realise that joining GA is incompatible with Ed's idea that I might gamble my way out of this, I honestly don't think I'd have the energy for that either. You need to be really on your game if you're thinking about screwing big money out of a bookie in a few days.

'Thanks . . . I know everything is a pain in the arse for you now . . . so thanks,' James says, like the gentleman he is.

'You've earned it.'

'As soon as you sit down in that room I'm sure you'll realise you've come to the right place.'

Maybe for the first time it strikes me that the people in that room may be the only people who don't despise me in some way, being too busy despising themselves. I should have figured that out before, but it's that old failing of mine again, the way it takes me so long to really understand things.

'They'll all look up to me in there. I'll be the main man,' I say.

It seems so obvious to me now. It seems like I might even enjoy being there with a load of like-minded assholes.

'I think you'll enjoy the fellowship. It's, eh, it's something that I know a small bit about myself,' he says.

'Ah, James . . .'

'I'm not a – perpetrator as such, more a victim. My father is an alcoholic, as we know. So my mother sent me to a few meetings of Al-Anon, sort of the youth wing, for people affected by addiction. I never kept it up but . . .'

The way he said that, I'm starting to wonder to what extent he has been counselled and therapied, to what extent he is more grown-up than I am. It makes me feel like the younger man or maybe, to be more accurate, the fucked-up adolescent.

'OK. I'm not being smart here, but you're driving on top of a fair few whiskeys,' I say.

'I'm not an alcoholic,' he says, as if I have said something very strange.

'I'm not saying you are. Just curious,' I say.

'That's OK. I drink too much from time to time but that doesn't make me an alcoholic. The thing about drink for me is that it doesn't really change me. I don't turn into someone else when I have the first drink, not like my father, who has one drink and it lights him up. Or maybe you, with the first bet . . .'

'Why would I go to a GA meeting when I can just listen to you?' I say.

'I did something really fucking stupid and irresponsible tonight, drink-driving, risking my licence.'

'Just to get something out of me?'

'Well, I did, didn't I?'

He doesn't sound smug, just smart, just professional. I

am starting to believe in him now, more so than when I felt that his main attribute was his large physical presence, his respectful manner.

'The whiskey is making you a bit bolder, James,' I say.

He lets out a big laugh. 'That's what it's for, John.'

There was another reason why James decided not to call a taxi. There's a large bungalow just up the road from where we are parked. James explains that it is the home of Brian Gill, the man we observed earlier in his shop. He figures I'd like to know that.

I study the house for a while, admiring it as a superior type of bungalow, one that has clearly been designed by an architect. But everything else I feel is just some ridiculous nervous energy from the night, and the drink, and what James has been saying to me, and what Ed was saying to me last night.

'If you check it out, in this region you could probably get to a GA meeting every day. I'll drive you if needs be,' he says.

'And this will work?' I say, in mordant style.

'I'll talk to our barrister, Maurice Field, tomorrow. Figure out a strategy.'

'Three, four years . . . that's the best we can do?'

'The best we can do . . . is the best we can do,' he says.

'Very good, James,' I say, impressed by his refusal to pander to my childish need to pick a number.

'This judge, O'Donnell. He's a regular on this circuit but I've not had dealings with him. He's said to be very bright.'

'Is that good?'

'We have to give him something, and you getting hooked up to Gamblers Anonymous in all sincerity really is something.'

'Will it work as well as paying back the money would work?'

'The two are incompatible,' he says, in that pretend-lawyer legal tone.

Which isn't exactly an answer to my question. And still, when I think about even the possibility of chipping away at this sentence, I don't feel as completely powerless as I have felt for a long time now, and again for a few minutes I don't want to kill myself anymore. And then that passes too.

James gestures towards the house we've been observing. 'There's one thing I know. The unfortunate man who lives in that house over there, I hear that the woman who was killed went to the same Sunday evening Mass as him and his wife, and actually went up and sat down in the seat next to him. Just sat there, for the whole Mass, and said nothing and then they all went home.'

'Ah, Jesus . . .'

'Tough.'

James takes out a packet of cigarettes. Seems he smokes the odd one, but he's able to control that too. He offers me one, and with the windows all up the car is soon filled with smoke, just like most of my world used to be, in the good times.

The heat and the smoke are getting too much. We have been driving and eating and drinking and thinking and talking for a long time. We head back around the town and out to the village, just to listen to the sound of the sea on the strand.

CHAPTER 11

I wake up in the damp bedroom of the caravan. The walls of this little room seem a bit more fragile than usual, as the caravan shakes with the November gusts of wind and rain. I stare at the black wet stains on the walls, my head still numb with whiskey, trying to figure out where I stand this morning with the gods, as if it wasn't entirely clear.

I am damned, I think. Still damned this Monday morning, just like yesterday and the day before and all the days to come. And then some ludicrous energy inside me that seems to operate outside my jurisdiction starts to do its familiar work.

Yes, I am damned, but not as damned as the journalist Jim

Hallahan is damned, that man who used to write a brilliant newspaper column, who was known to the general public as a most admired practitioner of his craft, but who in yesterday's papers became known mainly for some insane relationship he is supposed to have had with a fifteen-year-old boy. They're talking about him on the radio now as a possible predator, where once they would quote lines from his work and sigh with satisfaction.

When I think about Hallahan this morning, I have this great urge to find out where he is and to visit him, to talk to him about his humiliation and my humiliation, because only men who have been humiliated as we have been have any true understanding of it.

I want to be generous towards him, to take the view that he had somehow been swept away by some ungovernable madness, that he needs forgiveness along with all the judgement. But then I question my own disposition in that deal, the fact that I have some skin in that game of forgiveness, and the fact that, in my madness, I have been more fortunate than he was.

I was not widely admired; I did not have such talent. My crime was not loaded with the terrible weight of underage sex; it was only money. Yes, when I think of Hallahan I can actually say, 'It was only money,' and it means something.

I didn't kill anyone and I didn't sexually abuse anyone and it was only money.

And so I get to thinking that it would actually be selfish of me to go to him. Even patronising. As if my form of leprosy is slightly less vile than his, and I feel good about that. And in that thought I lose the impulse to be generous, just to identify in some tangible way with a human being who is in the shit. I'm sure I am not the only one, that there are friends of Hallahan who have let that impulse get away from them in these last few days.

I am not the only one – in itself that line is a way of getting around it, of feeling no different from the next guy in this regard, and that makes it all right.

Yesterday too, I decided to kill myself, and it felt good. And then, in the company of James, I went off that idea.

I decided to help myself, or to seek help, as they say, for my addiction, for my case. And this morning I'm still intending to do that, and it feels good. Just as good as it felt yesterday when I decided to kill myself.

Later in the day it might be the other way round. How I wish that I could just feel the same way most of the time, that I could either give myself honestly and enthusiastically to the work of rehabilitation, or that I could tell them all to go and fuck themselves, and leave them with just my body washed up on the strand, leave them to find someone else to vilify.

It's still an even-money chance that I will go that way, and as a gambler, I always tried to avoid the even-money chances, the heads or tails. I needed the chances to be better than that to get my juices running.

And then there's another destination, which doesn't involve either oblivion or healing. It's the place I go to sometimes, the place of my youth, of my spirit, when I knew the meaning of life, when I heard all the deepest secrets of the universe blaring out of the jukebox in the amusements, on any evening in July.

I can never get that out of my head. No matter how many troubles are sent to distract me and to consume my days, no matter how many people are on my case, I am being drawn back there, and I feel there must be some very good reason for that and here it is: I feel it is the most exquisite of all the cruelties devised by the baleful gods, the one they set aside for those they hate most fervently.

By coming back to the village, I have made it so easy for them to torment me in this way, to fill me with longing for things that are gone.

Ed Brennan was in that place with me, and Annie Campbell. Ed has become grotesque now, to the world, but he knows and I know that he is not grotesque, that the drink just got him and that something before that made it easier for the drink to get him, just some feeling of failure on his part, perhaps all that desolation because he could never be a musician. Not a professional anyway, at best a part-time drummer in some trio that did pubs and weddings, which was no good, really, for a man of his sensibilities.

He did not have the talent he needed, or the luck he needed, so he went to the bad. He did not get to play with a proper band, and it crushed him. And if you knew that, as I know it, you would find it hard to see him just as a grotesque.

In fact, he sees much around him that is grotesque, among the respectable people of the town. He has their number.

And as for how he sees me, well, he knows me. That's all.

We know one another in ways that nobody else knows us, certainly none of the bastards who would place themselves high above us in their own estimation.

So as I make it out of bed here, in the middle of the day, I have the inclination again to wear some of my best clothes, my dark brown cashmere jumper, a grey silk shirt, my most expensive jeans. I get them out of the wardrobe where they have not yet been ruined by the damp, not completely. I get dressed and then I stand looking at myself in the mirror for a while, trying to get some sense of who I am or who I was.

I have twelve days now, until my trial.

Ed gives me a fright the way he pushes open the door of the caravan and puts his head around it without knocking. It's not just his sudden presence in the room, it's the way he seemed to emerge from my semi-conscious, like I thought about him and he appeared.

'I was worried about you,' he says.

Today he looks more affable in his largeness. Or maybe just more sober. His blotches seem less angry.

'That's nice,' I say, gathering myself for what may become another session. Reminders of the last one are still to be seen on various surfaces in tall glasses with cigarette butts drowned in the remains of the gin and tonic.

I am about to thank him for the fine gesture of leaving that two grand in betting money for me, but I don't have the energy yet for the negotiations that may ensue.

'It is nice . . . it is nice to have somebody worry about you. Nobody worries about me, do they?' he says.

He sounds accepting of that, not bitter. I find myself admiring the leather jacket he is wearing today, a dark brown one with buttons rather than zips, more the jacket of a rock'n'roll manager than of a fat, middle-aged punk. And he is wearing jeans that fit his bloated middle so perfectly they might have been tailored. I am also forming the view that his hair, such as it is, may not after all be dyed brown, or if it is, that he's done it very well. Both of us, it seems, are hanging on to that sliver of self-regard, the habit of looking sharp that we got into when we were wild with hope. One of our good habits.

'I was thinking there about Jim Hallahan. You heard about that?' I say.

'Do you know him?'

'No.'

He looks a bit puzzled for a moment, as if he thinks I should know Hallahan. As if our ruination has connected us in his mind.

'Nobody knows anyone,' he says.

'They're getting to know me quite well,' I say.

'I texted you earlier. No response,' he says.

'I guess I slept through it. Hungover after a night out with your son.'

'Us boys,' he says, taking a packet of Rothmans out of his top pocket and offering me one. I take it in the spirit of a man who has been given a grave diagnosis and who figures that the rest of him isn't really worth preserving. I root around in a cupboard for a saucer to serve as an ashtray, a move that in this place has a hint of bourgeois pretension.

'You boys . . . Look, I don't know if you told me this already, but is it you who isn't talking to him or is it him who isn't talking to you?' I say, taking a light directly off his cigarette, just like we used to do.

Ed has a deep drag, as if he's trying to remember something that happened a long time ago. 'It's just the way . . .' he says.

In his voice there is no sense of regret or frustration, more of calm acceptance that this is how things can turn out, whether you want it or not, and there's no point in complaining. 'Right,' I say.

'The truth is, we don't really know one another that well,' he says.

In another situation I might suggest they do something about that – they might be surprised how these things can work out – but I don't really have the time for that now, for someone else's troubles. If that's the way it is with them, that's the way it is. But he did come to me through James, sending that text. I guess he didn't have a number for me but he could have come up here at any time.

'Still, you did him the courtesy of texting him, asking would it be OK for the two of us to meet?' I say.

'The courtesy, as you call it, was to you. I know you like that kind of shit,' he says.

'And it just happened to include him?' I say.

Ed retreats to the back seat of the caravan and sits down, spreading his arms in a pose like that of a corporate swine on the front cover of his autobiography. 'You don't have children of your own so maybe you don't understand,' he says.

'I defer to you there.'

'It is possible to have very little contact with your children and to feel nothing about it – nothing bad anyway – and for them not to feel bad about it either.'

'Then again, you'd get roughly the same result by not having children at all,' I say.

He smiles indulgently, even paternally. 'But you can help them, in your own way.'

'I hear they wouldn't take your money,' I say.

He is not offended by this, by anything it seems.

'You've got me thinking now that maybe in the end I'm helping you both equally, James and you. Did that occur to you?'

'It didn't occur to me that you were helping at all,' I say.

He thinks about this, then breaks up laughing. 'That's good, Johnny,' he says.

'And maybe we don't need any help. I'm starting to think that James might be good.'

He considers this with some seriousness. 'Good as he may be, good as any of us are, we can all be better,' he says.

'You don't rate him, do you?' I say.

'I told you, we don't really know one another that well.'

'He impressed me last night. We had a spin around the town, checking out some of the good burghers you mentioned,' I say.

'Must have given you a laugh.'

'It's a howl, Ed.'

He lies down on the seat, smoking, holding forth. 'I was harsh on you the other night,' he says.

'A bit.'

'Hadn't seen you in so long. Pent-up . . .'

'You were not wrong,' I say.

Ed shifts his position to study me for a while, a look in his eye that could be compassion. He sighs like a man who is reluctantly moving from a discussion of light topics to more troublesome matters. 'We have both been wrong, about many things,' he says.

'I guess we have.'

He raises himself onto his elbow, like this is important. 'Or maybe we just got things the wrong way round. You know what I was listening to in the car on the way up here? I was listening to the soundtrack of *Saturday Night Fever*, I swear to God. All that Bee Gees shit. Did we know at the time how good that shit was? I don't think we did, Johnny. I don't think so.'

His eyes are fixed on some distant place, as if he's trying to remember exactly how things were.

'I think I knew they were great, Ed,' I say.

'Fuck off,' he says, like I have barged in on a moment of great sensitivity. He is sitting up now, still probing this new discovery of his.

'Sorry,' I say.

'I really can't recall . . . did we love *Saturday Night Fever* and all that great pop music, or did we not love it?' he says, still concentrating on that faraway spot.

'I think it was like this. I think it was just the people who loved that music that we didn't love, which was just about everyone, I guess.'

Ed smiles in recognition. 'We laughed at those people. Remember how we laughed at that guy from the town who won the Disco Dancing World Championship or something?'

'Sure we laughed at him, but did we laugh at Travolta? I can't remember either,' I say.

The talk stops. I listen to the wind and the rain beating against the caravan.

'I think we did laugh at him too. I think we hated all that disco shit. In which case maybe neither of us was as smart as we thought we were.'

His words suggest that he is being self-critical, yet his tone is forgiving, certainly forgiving of himself. It could be that Ed the happy drunkard just can't recall things rightly anymore: he's trying to put it together and he's missing a few pieces. Or maybe he's like me, realising that time doesn't work the way he thought it did, that there are moments when he, too, seems to be living his life backwards. Maybe the two of us will eventually understand what everyone else understood when they were fifteen.

'We liked Elton John before anyone else did,' I say, to give us our due.

'And then we stopped liking him for some reason.'

'True,' I say.

'Maybe we got that one wrong too.'

'Maybe we did . . .'

'After *Yellow Brick Road* he owed us nothing,' he says.

CHAPTER 12

He gets a spasm of laughing, which starts me off too. He eases himself off the seat, like he is protecting his back, like he is afraid that the laughing will give him a slipped disc.

It is the laughter I heard from him before, the laughter of his original self. He gets to the kitchen counter and stands there doing something on the laptop. I'm thinking he must be visiting his online betting account, to see how I am doing with it, but then the music starts, the piano and then the voice of Van Morrison singing 'Linden Arden Stole The Highlights'.

Ed seems to me in this moment like some sorcerer who

has control of time, who by working his machine can return both of us to some distant pleasure we knew, that we shared.

'Linden Arden Stole The Highlights'.

I understand now that he's found it on YouTube, but I can't make it over to the kitchen to have a look at Van singing it, or at the montage, or at whatever they've done to it, because I am not here at all. I am gone.

'Linden Arden Stole The Highlights'.

I heard those words for the first time from Ed, when we were walking down to his place late one night after some teenage party we'd left early. We were drinking more than anyone else and we were finding out that most of the people we knew didn't seem to like the things we liked, or feel the way we felt. Though it must have been worse for me because Ed, of course, had a girlfriend, which one I can't recall right now. One of those normal girls he was still able to get along with, before they started drifting away from him too.

'"Linden Arden Stole the Highlights",' he said, as we were walking past the big garage where they kept the bus that brought the people from the village into the town. It is fixed in my mind that that was where we were and that was what we were doing when he said those words, not knowing that in just naming a song he was bringing something into my consciousness that would still be able to lift my heart in these last days of mine out here.

Yes, he was always getting there just a bit before me, with his trips to the North, so I remember I wasn't surprised he had brought back this new thing he was talking about, the album Van Morrison had made back in 1974 called *Veedon Fleece*.

Then he started talking about this song, 'Linden Arden Stole The Highlights', which he said was strange because it was only about two and a half minutes long, but which I found strange because it was such a beautiful title, whatever it meant. It sounded so good that it hardly needed a song attached to it, even a short one.

But the song, as I found out when we got back to Ed's place, with a few bottles of beer we had taken from the party, was more than beautiful. I am hearing it now and it is still impossibly great, maybe even the greatest thing that Van has ever done, which would make it beyond great, beyond all that we know in this life. I am hearing it, this story of a man's life, the story of his soul all done in two and a half minutes, and then it's over.

'We were right about that one,' Ed says.

I go to the counter, not to look at YouTube, because I couldn't take that, but to lift another of Ed's cigarettes from the packet he keeps in his top pocket. What is one more addiction, indeed, when you've got a collection like mine?

He lights me up, as if eager to keep me going on this exciting new phase. I take a drag of the Rothmans and it feels normal now, to be smoking again at the start of the day. 'Linden Arden Stole The Highlights' has made we weak.

'Thanks, Ed,' I say, with a hint of accusation.

'Yeah, we were right about that one,' he says again, and I sense this sadness creeping into his voice, like he has opened up his own store of melancholia.

What chance did we have, after all, once we had heard the voice of Van Morrison singing 'Linden Arden Stole The Highlights'? For all our smartness we were two sensitive young men and we had given ourselves to something so pure and so fine that it changed us. All the more because we had found this thing ourselves, this soul medicine.

And partaking of it, on that night and on many other nights, we found ourselves in the land of the ever-young where we were bound to devote ourselves completely to such fine things. And deep down we knew the deal, that if we ever came down from that place, if our feet touched the ground, we would lose it all and we would become three hundred years old. But we were too drunk on it to care.

I sense that Ed understands this, that he maybe understood it before I did, giving him time to accept it, to stop fighting it. But still he can't stop himself playing that song again, playing 'Linden Arden' . . .

'I met this guy who knew Van quite well,' I say.

'Oh, yeah?' Ed says, like he really wants to know more.

'Nice fellow called Don, very funny guy. He was with a girl who knew a girl I knew.'

'Great,' Ed says, like he admires me for all these interesting people I have known.

I am letting the ash from the cigarette fall onto the floor of the caravan. It's probably the hangover from the whiskey but my brain feels disconnected from the present tense, soaked with these visions that seem to have stayed somewhere in my head, when so many other things have disappeared.

And on this half-drunk morning even these visions, which seem so clear to me, bring their own doubts. Was it really down there at the bus station that I first heard Ed talking about 'Linden Arden', and why would I remember that when I have forgotten so many other things? Was it really such a moment?

I recall now a sensation I used to experience back then, whereby I would have this heightened awareness for a minute or two, a feeling that I had no idea who I was, that I was existing in this body and yet a stranger to it. That I was outside myself. Maybe it is a normal thing that happens to everyone from time to time until their personality is more developed, or maybe it was some signal from the purest part of my being that I would always be deficient in some way, that an element was missing, that I could never be whole.

It was a thing I could never talk about to Ed, not because it was too profound but because it was as insubstantial as it was profound. Of its nature it was obscure, like some reminder from another dimension that there would always be this part of you that would remain unknown, even to yourself.

The music has transported me so far away from my immediate circumstances that I can't even be bothered to put out my cigarette in the saucer that Ed is using, so I stamp it out on the old carpet. I am remembering another thing about Don, the man I knew who knew Van.

'Don split up with that girl and he got very down. Tried to kill himself,' I say.

'The funny guy?' he says, engaged with the story, indifferent to my stamping out the cigarette on the floor.

'The funny guy. He borrowed a car and drove it up to a forest in the Dublin mountains. He attached a tube to the exhaust and he sat there in the front seat with the engine running, drinking a bottle of whiskey, waiting for the end. The fumes overcame him, or maybe it was the drink – anyway, it all went black for him. And the next thing he knows he's still sitting in the car but all around him there is mist, a thick mist that puts the thought in his head that he must have died and gone to Limbo.'

'Limbo,' Ed says, just the word making him laugh.

'So this is what Limbo is like, he's thinking, getting really terrified now, because he'd never believed in Heaven or Hell or any of that. This is Limbo, this misty place in which you just have to wait, maybe forever. And he's got a really bad headache . . .' I take another cigarette from Ed, enjoying his absorption in my tale.

'It takes him a while to figure out that he's still alive, that this is just the morning fog all around him, that he had conked out but the fumes hadn't killed him because the car had run out of petrol.'

Ed drums his fists on the counter in delight. 'Run out of petrol!' he hoots.

'I think it was the oil crisis,' I say.

'It just wasn't meant to be,' he says.

'Not that time. He had another try about ten years later, put his head in the oven. That worked.'

Ed is laughing at the good of it all, or the good as he sees it. 'Another woman did him down?' he says, handing me the whole packet of cigarettes as a kind of reward, gesturing to me to keep them.

'The same one, I think. That was the feeling anyway, among those who knew him.'

'Fucking Limbo,' Ed says, savouring the image again.

'He was a bit like you. A failed musician,' I say.

Ed looks down at the laptop again, to give 'Linden Arden' another run. 'Really?' he says, unoffendable.

'This was our song, baby,' I say, sucking at the cigarette.

'I guess it was, too,' Ed grunts, but he is off on some other trip. His leg is starting to twitch, like his body has realised it's time for a drink. Then he laughs, not a twisted or sordid sound but one of mirth. And he starts mumbling to himself, as if for a moment he is unaware that anyone else is there. He switches off 'Linden Arden' and starts clicking. I can't see what he's looking at but I'm guessing it's the betting website. Then he speaks, still looking at the screen. 'It . . . could . . . be . . . so . . . fucking . . . great,' he says.

I can sense he's having another run at this betting marathon idea. 'Let it go, Ed.'

'So great,' he says, still chortling at the wild possibilities he sees.

'I really want to thank you for leaving that two grand in there for me. I was very moved by it. But I'm done.'

'It was my idea too – wet brain and all,' he says, with a note of pride.

'Well, you mentioned it, and then you fell into a coma.'

'Listen.' He laughs again, this time with just a hint of menace.

'I made a commitment to James last night that I'll sign up with Gamblers Anonymous,' I say.

He goes quiet for a while, giving me a bit of that passive-aggressive thing he was so good at when we were young. Then: 'You'd had a few drinks . . .'

'Leave it,' I say.

He slaps his own head in frustration. 'Gamblers A-fucking-nonymous,' he says.

'I'm out of the game. All I do now is punt a few bob to buy fish and chips,' I say.

'So you're not out of the game,' he says, seizing on any opening.

'I'm finished, Ed.'

'But if you had money . . .' he says, the frustration starting to burst out of him in the form of sweat.

'I'd buy a lot of fish and chips with it and a few pints. And maybe a new pair of shoes.'

'No, listen to me,' he says, coming over to me, taking a cigarette from the packet, his hands shaking as he lights it.

'No, Ed,' I say.

'Listen to me. It can be done, right? It's not beyond your capabilities?'

I am trying to wave him away but I can feel the first drop of adrenalin hitting a familiar place. 'I'm going to jail, Ed. I'm finished. I agreed with James that the best thing I could do is go to these meetings of Gamblers Anonymous. It would look good and it might even do me good.'

He is shouting now: 'But if you won a load of money and you could pay back some of the sad bastards whose money you stole . . . would that not look good? Would that not do you good?'

Horribly, there is still something in what he says. I have defended myself on the grounds that I just needed more time and everything would have been all right. Now I could prove it, and all I'd have to do is get out of this hole using the same shovel I used to get into it in the first place.

'In theory I could pay it back. In practice it's too much – millions when you add it all up,' I say. And there are some technical issues about bookies accepting vast amounts of money out of nowhere from a former winner, a guy who used to be good. Which should kill this discussion, but also shows that I am at least considering the ways and means.

'Not completely beyond you, I imagine, given a fair wind,' he says.

'The reason I'm here is I lost the ability to win. I just lost it,' I say.

'You just ran out of money, mate. That's all.'

'It was more than that. I ran out of hope.'

'Well, you can get it back, can't you? If you have the money the hope will come.'

He's working at my weakest spot, the fucker. He's arrived at the dead centre of the gambler's addiction, that endless supply of hope.

'I've promised James I'm going to the meetings. I'm going,' I say.

He pauses, as if exhausted by the effort of trying to explain these simple things to me. 'Say you win a load of money,' he starts again.

'I made a promise. That has to mean something.'

'No, it fucking doesn't.'

'It broke me, Ed. It sounds like a great laugh but it broke me, losing so much to those bastards . . . those fucking bastards . . .'

'So you're going to these meetings and then you're going to jail . . .'

'And more meetings in jail. They do that now,' I say.

'You're going to listen to James and not to me?' he says.

'Incredible as it seems,' I say.

He knows I've got him there, but he's not stopping. 'If I was this judge, right, I'd really need something pretty strong to start slashing away at your sentence and I'd look at it this way. A guy can swear off the gambling for a while and say he's going to meetings and he's found the Lord and he's doing counselling and all that fucking bullshit . . . but a pile of actual money put down on the table, that's evidence, buddy.'

He is so forceful: it's like for him there's a moral dimension to it, in the opposite sense to the usual one. He is convinced that good things can only be achieved through the path of vice. Whatever gives us the most pleasure is clearly the right thing to do – 'us', in most cases, meaning him.

'And there's only one problem,' I say.

'Those voices have got into your head, telling you that you need help, you've got a disease . . .'

'I might lose, Ed. I might lose. That's the problem. I might lose.'

He seems winded by this. Still, he tries to recover. 'You gotta know it could go the right way too,' he says.

'You gotta know the difference between seven years and three years, that's all,' I say, deliberately going for the low estimate of three.

He stands there looking at me, like he is trying to establish for sure that it really is me. It seems like he is going to explode with frustration. 'You don't know anything about yourself, do you?' he says, like it has fully dawned on him at last.

'Seven years is more than three years. I know that,' I say, getting weary of the fight.

'I mean, you still think you're right about everything,' he says.

'We did this,' I say.

'I mean, you don't know anything all. You really are a terrible fucking . . . asshole,' he says.

'We did this too,' I say.

'No, I don't think so . . . I don't think we've established just how wrong you can be, what an . . . asshole,' he says.

I felt he was wanting to go with 'eejit' again there, in fact I know he was, but he pulled back. 'Pushing an open door, Ed . . .'

He moves back to the laptop, typing something, contemplating whatever is on the screen. He folds his arms and leans over the counter, talking to me but not looking at me. 'Annie Campbell. Did you ever Google her?' he says.

'Knock it off.'

He does as I ask, holding up his hands in an exaggerated gesture of apology. 'Forgive me, for I am being an asshole too,' he says, still struggling to contain himself.

'I never Googled her because she's nothing to me now,' I say.

'She was,' he says, almost soothingly.

'She might have been.' I'm reluctant to concede anything to him.

Ed places his arm round my shoulders, like I am more to be pitied than blamed. He looks away as he speaks, as if this is making him nervous. Which in turn is making me nervous. He's acting like he really, really doesn't want to tell me this but it just has to be told.

'There was a kind of a party round at my place – records, bottles of beer, two kids sitting together with backs to the wall . . .'

'You're talking about me and Annie.'

'It's a bit hazy.'

'Then just leave it.'

'It probably was you and Annie.'

'You'll tell me anyway,' I say.

And he resumes his story, looking away again, closing his eyes, as if somehow this will make everything clear to him. 'We've got a free house so people can use the bedrooms upstairs. She gives him the signal, squeezes his hand or something, she leaves the room . . . she's gone for five minutes, ten minutes . . . He doesn't get it . . . He doesn't go after her . . .'

'You're talking about me.'

'OK, OK. Either you didn't pick up on the signal or you just weren't aware of it because you were listening to this great music – "Linden Arden Stole The Highlights" – sitting there, just listening . . .'

I should be heartbroken by the scene he describes, except I think he really is talking about someone else, not about me. 'I don't remember it like that,' I say, and in truth I barely remember the scene he describes at all.

He lets go of my shoulders and reaches for a relaxing smoke. 'You probably wouldn't want to remember it,' he says.

'Maybe because it's bullshit,' I say.

'Denial . . . denial is good,' he says, repeating one of his themes.

'I remember something that happened, or that didn't happen, in the cinema with an Elvis picture. Not at your place.'

'I saw it happening – saw you sitting there, listening,' he says.

'You have been pissed for a long time,' I say.

'That is true.'

'So maybe she was just out making a long phone call to her mother,' I say.

'But I heard about it too. Annie talked about it.'

This darkens it for me, because I can imagine that happening. I recall that women were always telling him things. I take one of his cigarettes, to help me through. 'She said nothing to me about it.'

'What can you say to an eejit?' He opens his arms in a gesture of helplessness, like I've left him with no option but to say that.

'So I'm sitting there listening to Van the Man while Annie is waiting for me?'

'That's what I saw . . .'

'And she tells you I missed the signals.'

'OK, I heard it from someone who heard it from her,' he says.

Now there is hope, and I build on it. 'And you didn't say anything to me at the time?'

'I didn't hear that bit for a while, a good while,' he says.

I laugh at this, and he can't help laughing with me. 'So

this is coming from some – some fucking clown who drinks in your place?'

'I have my own memory, you sitting there, and "Linden Arden" playing – most of that side of *Veedon Fleece*, actually.' He snorts.

'I don't have that memory,' I say.

'Maybe I'm wrong so,' he says, not insincerely.

'But thank you for your honesty,' I say.

He takes the barb with a grin. 'Then again you are such an – asshole, I'm inclined to think that maybe I'm right.'

He is working the laptop again. 'I can't find her on the internet . . . I mean, for fuck's sake, how many women from Ireland called Annie Campbell become police inspectors in Canada?' He taps away at the keys, getting agitated.

'Maybe you're wrong about that too,' I say.

CHAPTER 13

No, I can't rightly remember that scene with Annie but that doesn't mean it's not killing me. I would say I have been destabilised by Ed's story, except I wasn't all that stable anyway. It's an hour since he left me here, and even after all that I said to him, I am getting the urge right now to start betting with his money.

I told him I was going to the meeting tonight, and I meant it at the time, but if the gambler did all the right things he said he was going to do, he wouldn't have a problem. I know of no books I can read that offer guidance to the gambler. I am not even aware of a line of official bullshit of the type that they've been putting out for years about drinking and drugging. Which is why, in the demented hour after Ed leaves me here with his online deposit, I am shifting my position every five minutes.

First I am logging on to Ed's internet betting account, the details of which he has furnished to me, along with the two grand that is already in that account, with more to come. If I need it.

But it would probably need to be a lot more than two grand. Even starting with five I would need a fantastic run of results to bump it up to serious money. I'm not sure if Ed understands just how hard it would be, that it might take something more in the neighbourhood of thirty grand to get me started for real.

But I'm interested enough to be looking at the runners and riders for the next race this afternoon at Southwell, to consider a proper investment in it, not the pennies I've been punting on these races just to stay alive. It is a terrible race, full of bad horses, yet this weakness running through my blood is telling me I will back the winner of this terrible race, maybe win a few grand, and that I will feel better as a result, and the way things are, I really need to feel better about something. I am about to let myself go by pressing the button that says 'Bet Now'. Then I feel a belt of nausea sweeping through me, as I recall again those weeks in the Coombe when it all went down, that titanic orgy of losing.

It's like I've been permanently sickened by it, that it's become a tumour in my stomach which is activated by any thoughts of serious gambling. The vileness of it stops me pressing that button, 'Bet Now', and then for a few minutes I am leaning again towards that meeting of Gamblers Anonymous.

I remember the vileness, too, of the bookies, those corporate cunts who had me as their guest at the Curragh on Derby Day, talking shit to them in their smart-casual executive box while they knew – ah, they knew so well – how much I was losing: they had soaked a few million out of me and I was chasing those losses, and still they kept pumping me for more, making me their guest at the Curragh so I could feel I was still a big guy, that it was all going to end well somehow, pumping and pumping and pumping me, while with their other face they held to that line of official bullshit about their policy of Responsible Gambling. Ah, they are such bad, bad men.

Three times I am about to call James, to tell him I'll be going to that meeting this evening in the old church hall. Three times I feel that when I say it to him, I will finally be committed, and my life, for all its failure, will at least have some shape. Even some companionship.

Because there are no books, there are no experts who know as much as the people in those GA rooms I have spent so many years avoiding. It is only the gamblers themselves who understand the primal energies of gambling.

Three times I look at that number, four times. I didn't even save James's name in my phone because I didn't want to get to know him that well.

Will I toss a coin?

Still I don't call James because now I feel there is a way through the nausea, the vileness, a way that still allows me to gamble. I have, after all, lost everything. And, yes, yes, even when I thought I'd lost everything, I found out I could always lose a little more. And some more after that. I have lost so much, in fact, that I may have moved into some protected zone that is beyond losing, so that when I look at that number '2000' at the top left-hand corner of the screen, I get a sense that what I am looking at there is a free bet.

I am still enough of a player to know that these are very favourable conditions in which to operate. It allows me to achieve that state of mind perfectly balanced between engagement and indifference. It is someone else's money, which reinforces that state of mind, a beautiful situation well known to Wall Street.

And if I feel my powers returning, if I can knock it out of the park a few times, I can see myself bringing along a great sackful of money to the old courthouse, which should certainly get me as light a sentence as anything that James is proposing. In the most extreme circumstances, I might not even need to go to that old courthouse at all.

I have a choice between James and his father. A choice between giving it all up, and going at it with a new sense of mission. A choice between the fellowship of Gamblers Anonymous, and the singular fervour of the uncured punter.

Or I could surrender completely to the persuasion of Ed,

and I could try both. Like James, I now have some idea of how these fellowships work so I am aware that, technically, all you need is the desire to stop drinking or drugging or gambling. That's it, just a desire to stop.

And I have that desire to stop.

The fact that I also have the desire not to stop is what has me here five times, six times, seven times, looking at that phone number for James, wondering how I could be considering such dishonesty, considering this crookedness, this programme of recovery and relapse, of abstinence and indulgence.

Am I overestimating the goodness of James? He is, after all, a solicitor. So he would understand, in a pragmatic way, that it doesn't have to be one way or the other, that if I was in a position somehow to pay back a proportion of the money, combined with a resolution to stop betting, one day at a time, it would be stronger than any position that has occurred to either of us until now.

It occurred to Ed, though, because he has long ago stopped making choices between good and bad, between right and wrong. Ed just looks at that list of all the good burghers of the town who want to have it every way, and he is liberated from any of those tough old-fashioned choices. Ed can call himself a happy drunkard, seeing no contradiction there, proud that he has risen above such conventional thinking.

Eight times, nine times, ten times I look at that number for James until I don't have to look at it anymore: I've memorised it.

I decide I will tell him exactly how it's going to be – that I will be embarking on a gambling binge, and attending meetings, regardless of the apparent contradiction. And then ... then I decide not to do that. Then I decide to lie to him. Yes, I will lie to him. I will tell him I am going to that meeting tonight, to keep him quiet, and I will say nothing about the gambling binge that I am starting maybe even before tonight. For what is James to me? He is not my son, he is not my saviour, nor is he some old friend with whom I soldiered. He is just some kid I hardly know who has been kind to me, or at least not unkind, probably because he doesn't yet know enough about the world.

So I am about to call James to tell him that lie.

But my voice, when I start to talk to him, doesn't want to obey me. It wants to obey some other command.

'I need cigarettes, James,' I say.

That is the truth: I need cigarettes. Ed, having given me his packet, took it away with him without thinking, and I, having dropped the habit so long ago, forgot to stop him.

'You don't want to go into a shop?' James says.

'I need to meet you anyway,' I say.

That, too, is the truth, coming out of me unplanned.

I arrange to meet him on the strand, out where the tide is coming in, an elemental place beyond the reach of the law, somewhere that isn't this rotting caravan, with the laptop with the betting website on it, a place that at this moment I would like to burn like a Hallowe'en bonfire, and not just the carpet – except the whole rotting shack is all so mildewed you probably couldn't burn it.

I will get my own cigarettes. I need them. I can't wait for James. I leave without even closing the door, let alone locking it, like I am trying to make these small gestures towards freedom before they bang me up.

I get a strong wave of fear running through me now at that thought, the prison-fear, a fear that is deepening all the time. I think of the contractions of a woman in labour, the way they increase in frequency and intensity, except at the end of that there is supposed to be the astonishing release of birth – for me there will be no such triumph.

So, when I get to the top of the main street and I walk into the mini-market to buy a packet of Rothmans I am prepared for any reaction on the part of the girl at the counter because, in truth, it is the least of my worries.

I hand my credit card to her, and as we wait a few seconds for the transaction to be processed, I detect a stiffening in her, a nervousness, but given the displays of contempt I have endured in other premises, I'll take that.

The important thing is that I have a cigarette in my mouth and I'm lighting it and inhaling, and it distracts me for a few seconds from the fear.

I walk down the promenade, and out towards the sea. I am going to meet James.

It is getting dark; the lights are on in the village. The tide is out a mile, there is nobody else out here walking the promenade, and with the wind and the rain of the morning gone now, it is a decent enough evening for November, cold but calm. I jump down from the promenade and start walking towards the tide. I expect James will see me out there.

Even in the more desperate moments of this desperate situation, there is something in me that is disgusted at the idea of getting help, having been self-sufficient for so long, relying on nobody else to stay ahead.

I am being drawn towards the river, which cuts across the sea about a thousand yards from shore, a thing I never understood as a child, a river that was part of the sea. We were paddling out here when I was about six, and my father had to carry me back to the shore when I stood on a big broken shell that sliced open the sole of my foot. He tied his handkerchief around the wound and brought me to the chemist on piggyback. I haven't been back to the river until today.

Seeking dry stretches of sand in some futile attempt to protect my shoes, I walk straight out towards the horizon, imagining England is just on the other side of the bay.

I reach the river. In the distance I can see that the tide is coming back in, maybe thirty minutes away. I see the lights of the houses on the far side of the bay, and I get the brief illusion that these are untroubled houses, untroubled lives, not like mine. Although I know that the truth may be very different, always that illusion comes to me first.

I can see James approaching now from the village, and when he joins me out here we will look to some kid on the promenade like two men in long black coats engaged in some obscure kind of work, a survey of the environment or some such, with no awareness that one of us will probably be in jail next week, for quite a long time. I want so much to be that kid on the promenade, which is who I was in the beginning. I want to be just about everyone else who is not me.

'Ed's fault,' I say, taking out another cigarette.

'Most things are,' James says.

As I hold the cigarette in my cold hand, I see that he is wearing black leather gloves, as if to illustrate which of us is the grown-up in this deal. 'I'm struggling,' I say.

'You did well last night. Gave me a lot.'

'I'm still going down,' I say.

He looks across the bay and nods, as if he is trying to imagine what going down would be like. 'Just get to the meeting,' he says.

'There's a few hours till then,' I say, thinking that in those hours I could conceivably win forty grand and lose it again, or just lose the two grand straight off.

'I'll sit with you, if you want.'

He'll sit with me. Maybe because I have lived in a state of such total self-interest and self-absorption for so long, it always surprises me when someone is simply being helpful, as James is being here. Especially when it might require him to stand guard over an addicted gambler in a hideous caravan, a thing which no lawyer would expect to do or would even consider doing.

It surprises me, this way of his, but it also disarms me, because I find it beautiful. 'Ed makes the case that I have nothing to lose by working that account. That if I get lucky and win a load of money that's great. The judge will see a large cash donation in much the same light as a last-minute conversion . . . maybe a better light.'

'You don't think that sounds a bit too neat,' he says, a statement not a question.

'Tell me what's wrong with it.'

'It's delusional,' he says.

'I know that. But, delusional as it is, tell me what's wrong with it.'

He smiles indulgently, as if he is being asked to explain something to a child. 'In a movie, maybe, it would work.'

'Maybe you can't relate to anything that's coming from Ed.'

'Maybe you're right.'

'And If I lose the two grand what does it matter? Who's to know?'

He gives me that smile again. 'A man of your experience . . . You still actually think that if you lost the two grand it would end there? That you wouldn't be tempted to go again? With Ed supplying the money?'

'But who's to know?'

I realise I am pushing it here, that I am sounding like Ed when he was war-gaming it with me this morning. But I am so far down in the hole, in every sense you can imagine, that I can't stop myself pushing it. And I feel that maybe James understands this.

'You yourself. You will know,' he says.

Again he has this way of confusing me.

'Right,' I say blankly.

He seems quite calm, standing there putting it up to me like this.

'I'll probably know as well, but mostly it's you,' he says.

'But I . . .' I start to babble. I'm thinking that he's talking like some kind of a clergyman, that the guy I thought was good last night may not be good after all.

'So why haven't you started betting with Ed's money already, if nobody's going to know?' he says.

'Because . . . because it fills me with disgust, I guess, in about a hundred ways . . . To go back there . . . to lose again . . . because I know it's delusional, all that . . .'

He seems to be waiting for me to elaborate on what 'all that' might be, but I can't describe it anymore. I described it to Ed, that feeling of being finished and broken and afraid of going back in there, and when I had described it, it didn't make me feel much better.

'Whatever it is, whatever it is that stops you, that's all you've got left,' he says.

'That and about two grand.'

He isn't interested in the numbers. 'Whatever it is that stops you, if you let that go, you have nothing.'

I guess I knew that, too, intuitively, but it helps me greatly that someone is standing here, laying it out so clearly for me. Even if he's sounding a bit like one of those Mormons who call to the door.

'Yes, sir,' I say, like a respectful American.

He shakes his head at the teasing, and smiles. 'Anyway, we need you to be genuine. Pretending doesn't work in court, I've found. If you're not really going to the meetings and swearing off the gambling in all sincerity it will show. There's a kind of a light that comes from people when they're being honest. That's what I think anyway.'

'I'm sure you're right. But by the time I get back to that caravan I may be sure you're wrong. Like I say, I'm struggling,' I say.

'Just get to the meeting,' he says, as if using some technique of repetition.

'Yesterday I wanted to kill myself. This morning I was listening to Van Morrison, and for about two and a half minutes I wanted to live forever. Then I felt like killing myself again.'

'So you were still suicidal,' he says.

He seems to like that one.

'Yes, our old friend the suicide.'

'It's got one thing going for it. It's true.'

'Can you get cigarettes in jail?' I say, lighting another. I want to ask him, Can you have a bet in jail?

'I'm going to tell you something now, and I want you to take it in the right way, OK?'

I am assuming he is going to point out another of the many defects in my character so I shrug. 'Sure.'

'I've been talking with Maurice Field, the barrister who'll be representing you in court, and we're seeing that judges are more inclined to be lenient on compulsive gamblers when it comes to sentencing. They're starting to see so many of these cases now. We've got Judge O'Donnell who is not the worst . . . we know there's no way you'll avoid a jail sentence, but we're thinking that we'll be pushing for it to be suspended . . . all of it.'

'Like . . . no jail time?'

'All of it suspended.'

'Right,' I say, a shot of hope running through me, and then out of me.

'Field agrees it's worth a shot.'

'But it probably won't happen. We're still looking at maybe three years at best with time off,' I say.

'That's it . . . and it could be dangerous too. Judges can be a bit bipolar, you know?'

'Like, he'll think we're taking the piss?'

'We're pleading guilty on all counts, of course, which will help.'

'Could you, eh, put it another way? Could you give me a rough idea of the odds on us getting a result here?'

'No. But I'll tell you one thing. They're a lot better than the odds on whatever crazy fucking shit that Ed has in mind.'

He seems a bit startled by his own little burst of profanity, but it is a righteous profanity.

'I'm really glad I called you,' I say. I am finding it as easy to be nice to him now as it was to be distant from him in the beginning. Yes, I am starting to think again that this guy is good.

'I'm getting an addiction counsellor to verify that you're entering a programme of recovery,' he says.

'And regardless of anything you've said here I just carry on as if I'm going to jail,' I say.

He nods with approval, like a doctor seeing signs that his patient is stirring out of a coma. It's nothing more than a hunch, I guess, but then we live by such hunches, by what we can tell from the aura of another person, whether we are looking at them across the poker table or across the wreckage of our own lives. Everything I am sensing from James tells me that, for a long time, he has been a creature of that thing they call reality, one who is driven by the ambition to achieve something of value in each day, not like me, and my kind, who wanted all the glory of winning, who thought you could get it all for free.

When I was his age I was already in love with gambling, and that affair still had a long way to run. And soon I'd be making more money at it than anyone I knew, not needing to deal with reality, or anyone who subscribed to it.

Yet I know, too, that he does not have contempt for me. I can feel that as clearly as I can feel the November cold. I can take it as a fact.

'Listen, John, you wouldn't be in prison with murderers,

you'd be in with white-collar guys,' he says, still steering me back towards those dire realities.

'I'll take the murderers, if that's OK,' I say, a joke he ignores.

'If you can show some sign that you're turning things around you'll get a lot of help,' he says. He doesn't repeat the possibility of me staying out of jail altogether. He just looks away to the tide, which is getting close.

'And how bad could it be with this judge? How long could I get?' I say.

'There's no good way of putting this. People out there really don't like you . . . They don't like what you did . . . and not just the people you robbed.'

There have been times when I have forgotten how much I am despised, an hour here or there when I forget I am the Ponzi Man, or I think that nobody gives a damn, and maybe that is a mechanism we have that protects us from disgrace, from the perfection of the logic that tells us to kill ourselves, to stop thinking about it, to just walk into the water and keep going.

Yet it still cuts me to hear him say this – just because it is him saying it. I have become accustomed to the universal contempt directed against me, but in this particular case I feel the need to fight it. 'You know it's not just black and white,' I say, thinking again about all those people who aren't coming after me because the money they gave me was less than totally legitimate, or just plain ill-gotten.

'But still . . .'

'I got unlucky too.'

'I know . . . I know. But you need to have the demeanour of someone who is stricken with guilt and shame. You need the judge to believe that you're taking this lying down.'

This is a grown-up person talking to me, and it always takes me a moment to adjust to that. We are smart, we gamblers, smart enough to know how the game is rigged, but too immature not to play the game in the first place.

He punches one gloved hand against the other, fighting off the chill of the sea. I probably wouldn't mind going to Cooney's with him right now, if that was possible, which it is not, and spending the night drinking with him, remembering the good things about growing up here. Though I have found that the good things tend to fade and get battered, like some old cassette tape, while the misfortunes we have suffered are always perfectly recorded and preserved, always ready to play.

I want it back, that old world I knew about a thousand years ago, a world without subterfuge. Without sizing everything up from twenty different angles. Without thinking too much and without knowing too much. Without gambling.

CHAPTER 14

The water is getting close to us now, as if the tides are suggesting a natural break in our conversation.

'Glad I called you,' I say.

'It's great that you called me,' he says.

'Yes.'

'I'm going to use that stuff about your charitable donations as well. Whether you like it or not.'

I don't fight it. Yes, it is great that I called him, that I did something which has given me a true guide to the contest that lies ahead of me, instead of just sitting up all night drinking gin and plotting, which is the usual *modus operandi* of us down-going men.

I think I can make it to that meeting now, without James baby-sitting me any further. I look across his shoulder to the bay and back to the village and I can imagine it abundant again. I don't feel like some broken-down punter, running down the days to the end of his life. I feel like I am hanging on to something.

I understand . . . I understand in a way I have not understood before that all these illusions have destroyed me, all these visions of a life without working and of winning, always winning in the end, have gone bad on me. And now all my tormenting visions of summer in this place have wasted me further, taunting me for all I have lost. Just when I desperately needed to be living in the present day, they were calling me back, visiting me all the time with sweet, sorrowful waves of regret. But I think I have finished with that now.

'Whatever it is that stopped me having that bet . . .' I say.

'That's all you've got left,' James says, repeating the lesson like a teacher to a slow learner.

'And if I let that go . . .'

'You won't let it go,' he says.

And he leaves me there, his good solicitor's shoes all messed up with the sand and the salt water, probably trying to get away from me before I bring bad luck by asking him to say again, one more time, that there is a possibility, a vague, outlandish, chimerical one but still a possibility that I may not spend any time in jail after all.

I want to shout some farewell to him but I am feeling quiet now. It is so unfamiliar that it seems to belong to some other version of me, maybe the one who delivered the mail, pushing that black post office bicycle down a lane, a little bit proud. I do not think I have felt such a quietness in my spirit since before I started going down, maybe even since I became a gambler, which is a very long time ago. Because the gambler is a man who is always at war, who must always keep going, maintaining the same face in victory and in adversity.

I am dizzy now, as if my body is just not able to cope with this quietness.

I start off in the other direction, back to the caravan. I look across to where the amusements used to be. I think about the boy I was, and the grown-up person I can become.

I slow down. I realise I have been hurrying for about twenty years, pushing it, maybe just trying to be on time for the first race.

So I am walking slowly now, and that feels better too. I will not be dragged around anymore by my own compulsions, by Ed's compulsions. I am not the centre of everything. I can walk as slowly as I like – I can even stand still and just listen to the sea. Wherever I am going I will get there eventually, at my own speed, in my own way.

I get the Super Ser started and inhale the smell of the gas, as if savouring a fine essence. I open the bag of chips I picked up on the way from the girl behind the counter who knows me enough by now to be thinking nothing of me. I don't mind that the chips are not made with potatoes, that they have no taste, that the best chips I ever had were those made by Mr Masarella before he punted the shop away. Maybe poor Masarella has never stopped – maybe he is still out there playing cards for serious money, deranged by his own illusions, but I have stopped.

'I've got it,' I say, not to myself, but out loud, like some character in a musical about to launch himself into an eleven o'clock number.

'I've got it,' I say again, as if it's some bizarre construction I am just trying out in a language that is not my own.

I've got it.

It feels as if the fault line in my personality has been put right, that I have heard what James is trying to tell me and have avoided what Ed has been trying to tell me, that something inside me has shifted and a form of peace has come. I have an inkling of some acceptance of myself now. I know what I have to do. I am going to lay down my troubles and I am going to this meeting, not because James or anyone else wants me to, but because I want to go there. I have a desire to stop gambling. Yes, I understand now what that means. I have a desire, a longing, to take this weight off myself, a tremendous need to concede defeat. I wish I could be there now, in that hall, but I will be there, in a few minutes.

I am starting to imagine what life might be like without gambling, without all my time and energy being consumed by the one quest, by rolling that rock up the hill again and again. I gave up everything for gambling – I gave up women for it.

This is so clear to me now, as clear as if I had sat down with the baleful gods one night when I was seventeen and done the deal – as if I had said to the gods, just let me be a gambler, a real gambler, and I will leave everything else to you. And the gods agreed to the deal, and they let me be a gambler, and now they have taken that away from me too. As they were always going to do.

I am thinking of Christina because she never had a chance. Maybe I have been harsh on her because in truth I know nothing about her, really, or about any woman. I know only this obsession.

I want to phone James to tell him these things, and to thank him too, because he started me off. He forced me out of my squalid incapability, he gave me that shove. I think I will send him a text now – *Thanks* – and I will phone him after the meeting, because I don't actually want to talk to anyone at this moment: I want to keep this to myself; I want to hear my own voice.

Where has it been, this voice of mine? So clearly now, I hear it informing me of what I must do, like the kindliest and wisest of mentors. Ah, that is another thing I lacked: I never had a mentor. I had Walter Jackson the bookie showing me his cheques in the pub on the way home from Fairyhouse; I had Mickey Tuite driving me into the dog track, then home with my pockets full of money and him full of whiskey; I had a whole civilisation assuring me that if you don't speculate, you won't accumulate. So I had to find that voice myself, and it took me such a long time, and so many things went wrong for me that I had reached the point of annihilation. And then as I walked back to the strand today in the dark I heard it and now I've got it.

I will not be doing this just to please somebody else, to appease a senseless system: I will be doing it out of my own fundamental need to get better. And, wondrously, if I do that, it will please other people anyway, and they will rejoice with me.

My consciousness, in these moments, seems to have grown greater than the universe, rendering all petty concerns of such small size they can no longer reach me. Disgrace cannot reach me because I have reached the end of all that: I am beyond the disdain of those who project their own unresolved shame onto me. I could empathise with them but I have no time for them. Their hostility towards me can have meaning only if I allow it to exist in the first place, if I let it in here, where I live. And I am not doing that anymore.

Jail cannot reach me now. It will be just a different set of circumstances, maybe even a refuge in which I can restore my energies and embolden my spirit because my heart is light: I am breaking free of this addiction, and I think that, wherever I am going now, I will spend my time in some fruitful way; I will appreciate the trip. There is now, it seems, so much time.

The time that is gone is gone.

That is how it seems to me now. I was given to unreality

until it devoured me, like some punter who doesn't realise that the races are over and everyone has gone home – and I, the punter supreme, of all people should not have been fooled by that one.

The life that is gone is gone. It was great for a long time until it turned to disaster. And it is over now, and I'm still here.

I have a desire now for some sort of gesture to mark my passing from the old life to the next, and I think I know what it must be – in fact, there would be no ceremony finer than the one I can perform in this room, with one action.

'Thank you, Ed,' I say, out loud again. 'Thank you, Ed, thank you, old friend, because you left that two thousand euro in your online betting account and you gave me the password.'

I start up the laptop and log in to Ed's account. There it is, two thousand euro in credit. One more time I will visit the site of my destruction, just to sign off, like a man I know who went out to have one last night of drinking, knowing he would never do it again. That afterwards his drinking would be done. I always felt he had done it the right way, that there is some need for a formal farewell, a ritual that will bring a decent end to the affair.

I gaze at all the markets on which I can have a bet, taking in the endless panorama of opportunity one last time, amazed and mortified that I let these bastards get the better of me, that I let them take me down.

I won't be doing that again because they have lost their

power over me. It no longer matters to me that I am any good at this thing; I am not proud of that anymore. I despise it all. And I hate the people who run this gambling business, hate them for their cynicism, their cruelty, the way they invite men into this idiot's parade only to take everything they own, take their lives.

I used to hate myself for letting them do that to me, but I think I am past that too. It is them now, it is just them I hate, with their 'fun' bets and their jolly geezers on the telly offering the odds on the next pope, their shit jokes. They are bastards, bastards every one of them, and I hate them on behalf of myself and every other poor weak man who has surrendered himself to them.

They will not get this money, which is not my money anyway, because they have lost me. Tonight they lose. I have the power now. I have got it.

I open up a market at random, one of the American races that they show on television at night for the chronically addicted, for all these smart men who have worked out every angle except the one that would reveal to them the certainty of their immolation.

I can see nothing there for me, nothing there for any half-sane person. I get out of that market with a click that takes me to 'My Account', and to the part of it that has the instruction 'Withdraw'. Like some medieval potentate applying the sealing wax to a solemn agreement I press the button: 'Withdraw'.

'You have successfully withdrawn 2000 euro,' the legend says.

In an instant that 2000 is on its journey back to Ed's credit card, and at the top corner of the screen the balance has been restored to zero.

'First, do not lose' was my core philosophy after all, and this time in not losing I feel, for one magnificent moment, as if I am the man who broke the bank in Monte Carlo.

CHAPTER 15

I walk down the main street of the village, remembering the names of the people who used to live in each house, still stuck in my brain from those three weeks when I was a postman.

I am again in the presence of that mystery, the fact that so many of the things I used to know in this life have disappeared from my head, yet these names remain, all in the right order too. Is it enough to say I must have been happy then? Is it not the case that we are more likely to hang on to our unhappy times?

Maybe it was not happiness I felt that Christmas, delivering the mail: it was more that I was growing up, that this was my first real job and I was doing it well. And maybe . . . ah, yes, maybe if I'd stuck to working, I would not be walking down this road again tonight. If I had not gone with my first wage packet straight to the bookie's and trebled it in the afternoon, I would not be walking down this road.

But I say that lightly, because I am hardly walking down this road at all: I am wandering there, like some contented child. Wandering, but I know where I am going.

I hear the sharp noise of my builder's phone. I read the text as I walk. It is James: *When you get to that meeting, it will change everything for you.*

Then he sends me another: *The best way to help yourself is to help other people.* It has the certainty and optimism of a man who is much younger than I am, much better in many ways. But I'll take it.

It sets off another recollection of something I had forgotten about until now, that around the time when I was eighteen and thinking of killing myself, for some reason that still escapes me, I also got this thought that I really wanted to go to Africa and become an aid worker.

Just the thought of getting out of this country and going someplace where I could forget about myself and where I might even be able to do some good made me feel ecstatic for a few hours, until I spoke to someone about it in a pub, and he explained to me that this is called 'doing a geographical' – thinking you can get away from your problems by going to live somewhere else. He added that the aid agencies in general are not really looking for emotionally unstable young men trying to escape their troubles – they're not the Foreign Legion. They want engineers, doctors, and so on.

I never had that thought again, but it gave me some inkling of the liberation that may be found in helping those less fortunate than yourself, a diminishing breed in my case, but still . . .

I turn left to walk up the steep tarmacked hill at the side of the church, where I used to go to Mass every Sunday until I was about fifteen, when I met Ed and we would go to his place instead. The likes of us eventually find our way back to the churches, except we don't use the front door anymore. Having hit the bottom, we come to the bare little halls around the back that we never knew existed, looking for just one place in which we might not be despised.

And some of us never get here at all.

I am still, in some obscure part of my soul, completely baffled to find myself arriving at this place on a winter's night, and I wonder what Ed is doing now, if he is happily drunk and if he will ever be doing anything else, and if that is the case, so what?

I am able to separate myself from the doings of Ed. I am floating again. I am carrying nothing with me tonight into this meeting except the knowledge that I have had my last bet, that I have taken this weight off myself and that, as a result, it is gone. How intoxicating it is to think that that could be done. That it might have been done at any time during the last fifteen years, but that I just didn't know it until now. I knew so many things, but not that.

The big oak door at the back of the church is ajar. Men who are addicted will always find a way to drink or to gamble, and it seems that we can find these places of fellowship, too, by instinct. There's a small sheet of paper on the door with the word 'Meeting' written on it, but there doesn't need to be.

I am two minutes early – in this, as in everything else, I am punctual. We gamblers tend to be, trained as we are to arrive before the start of the first race, always worried that we might miss something – sometimes I wonder how much grief I could have spared myself if I'd been just five minutes late for everything I did.

There are eight people in the room, seven men and one woman. Most of them are standing around a small table, drinking tea and eating biscuits. The others are standing with their backs to the radiator, observing me but probably paying more attention to the struggle to get warm. They see me coming but there is no big reaction, no double-take: my arrival here is entirely normal and appropriate. Even in a room with my own kind, I naturally assume the defensive position. But, then, none of these people would regard their personal catastrophes as being any less impressive than my own. In here we are all losers, except now we know it.

I am introduced to the group, all the names coming at me too fast, first names only, of course, Paul, Donal, David, Tony – I couldn't remember the others even five seconds after I heard them. The woman, well-groomed and in her thirties, is Karen. I would say she had something to do with running a business and defrauding it to pay for her casino losses, probably a dumb hunch on my part because I rarely associate sports betting with women – something about the need to be proved right about the result of a race or a match always seems to me essentially a weakness of the male ego. But I don't doubt I will be wrong about this too, when I hear Karen's story.

'You've come to the right place. This is a good meeting,' Paul says, shaking hands with me.

I am surmising that Paul, a strongly built, smart-looking man in his mid-thirties, might have worked in a bank and got through a lot of people's cash backing losers in the betting office next door. I will soon find out because he's chairing the meeting. He tells me he is the chair as he pours me a mug of tea, with milk and sugar. I like him immediately. He starts to explain how the meeting will work, that he will spend about ten minutes at the start reading from *The Big Book of AA*, the founding text of all the fellowships, and then he will relate his own story of how he got here.

'If you want to know my story I could tell you some of it tonight but you'll probably see the true version in *The Irish Times* in a few days' time,' I say.

No, it is not hilarious yet it gets a spontaneous laugh from all the guys, who have gathered around me in a way that feels welcoming and even protective without being creepy.

They're really not over-interested in me, just encouraging. I think I like them all.

Two are younger than the others, probably hot-shot online poker hounds, who have won tournaments in their time and brought four hundred grand home from a week in Vegas, then taken it all back again, along with another four hundred of their own. For luck.

I figure they were good, maybe even as good as I was, and the house still beat the shit out of them, and here they are now, drinking tea and eating biscuits.

Paul takes the chair and starts to read from *The Big Book*. I am sitting in the second row, but I am not really listening to him. I know what he's talking about, these ideas about seeking the help of 'God as we understand him', leaving a bit of wriggle-room in the words after 'God', about finding your Higher Power, because willpower alone will not do it. I am thinking mainly about the three words on a little cardboard sign on the table in front of him. 'Keep It Simple.'

It seems such a beautiful idea to me now, keeping it simple. All that I have in my life are complications, and there is much that is outside my control. I am so weary from it all, yet I am luxuriating in this idea that life may one day be simple for me, as simple as sitting in this bare room for an hour with a life of gambling behind me.

Paul was into sports betting, as I suspected, but he was actually doing all right at that, until he started playing blackjack online while he was waiting for a match to finish or a race to start, using the instant games of pontoon to keep himself wired, as the mania grew inside him.

He got into the property game, recognising it as a source of easy money and of betting opportunities on a large scale, the sort of bet that has no downside. You just buy a house and a few months later you sell it for about thirty grand more, and you keep doing this forever. And he was getting on all right at that too, well enough to hide the losses that were building on the sports and the online games of cards. And then that world disappeared one day, leaving only the losses. Leaving Paul with the prospect of retrieving those losses the only way he could, which was by doing exactly what he had done to acquire a lot of them in the first place. He knew it was all getting away from him – he was feeling that fear. He had a wife and two children.

Now I'm feeling the smallest squeak of resentment that I am sitting in this room alongside people with whom I can identify completely, and still I am the only one going to jail. I kill that thought, because I don't actually know for sure if all these people have stayed out of jail and, anyway, such bitter notions are only dragging me back to a place that I never want to see again, a place that is just too complicated for me, for any man.

I'm keeping it simple here. I have come to the right place. I have an urge to share, to explain how I got here, but, like I said, I figure they all know my story anyway. I am enjoying just being here, like someone who wants to hear the music without getting up to dance. I guess I've always been that way.

I have an urge to share something about being out at the river today with James, and how that moved me to some other dimension, but that, too, feels a bit much on a night when I need to lay everything down and leave it there.

It has moved me to hope, this new state of being I have found, and that is dangerous for me. So I'll just leave it there, yes, that is what I will do.

And I think of James, who pushed me into this, who knew what I needed so much better than I did myself. But I got here, in the end. I got here.

All I have to do now is to keep coming to these meetings, and finding this simplicity every time. Yes, they have meetings in jail and, yes, I am comforted by this. Just the thought of spending this hour every day with my fellow offenders is itself a kind of Higher Power.

I was right about the two young guys: they are victims of their own early brilliance at poker. They have trophies at home for winning tournaments, and now they are living one day at a time, with no action.

No action today, and no action tomorrow.

I didn't need to be Lieutenant Columbo to be right about those guys, but still I was right about them, as I have been right about almost everything. I don't think I'll ever lose that.

Turns out we have quite a range at this meeting. Karen was raised in the town but was bright enough to move to

London in her late teens to deal in stocks and shares, bright enough to be making half a million a year by her twenty-fifth birthday. Now she sits two chairs down from me, beside a beaten-up guy who is also from the town and had the disease in such a pure and deadly form, he spent all his days pumping coins into slot machines in some hideous arcade.

We're all the same tonight, we're all free, or at least we have some sense of what that might be like. Karen's life did not turn out as she imagined, yet she has this calmness about her. Usually someone who is as highly groomed as she is radiates a kind of anxiety, which comes naturally from the fact that they've spent too much time worrying about what others might think of them. Karen gives the impression that she is beyond such concerns, that when she was getting ready to come here tonight, she was doing it just for herself.

When the hour is done, Paul beckons me and tells me there's another meeting here in two weeks' time. I may not be around these parts in two weeks' time, which sends a jab of panic through me. I had felt so peaceful in this room, lulled into thinking there might be another meeting tomorrow night, and every night after that.

It seems to take so little for things to get complicated again. Paul gives me a list of other meetings in the town and in the county, working out that I could get to one each night I am at liberty, suggesting that I would need roughly a meeting a day in the early stages of recovery. He seems to assume I can drive to them, and I can't tell him otherwise. I have no idea why I can't tell him – it's not like he would be judging me for not having a car – I just can't get the words out.

I think again of James, who may have to bring me to these meetings. With him I have no pride.

I am walking down the hill away from the church, the same hill that I walked down every Sunday, its steepness making the release from Mass more exhilarating. Now it's pumping a few more endorphins into me as I pick up speed near the bottom, almost losing control and running out on the road. Turning towards home, I look at my phone. There's a message from Ed. It says, *Bad luck Johnny.*

It takes me about a hundred yards of walking with my heart banging against my ribs to work out that Ed would have access to the online account from which I withdrew the money before I left the caravan. It is, after all, his account.

And what he doesn't understand is that I haven't had a bet and lost the money: I have refrained from betting altogether and, as a result, I have broken even. Which would put me near the front rank of punters on this night or on most nights. Not that he would see it that way, but he does not sound too down about his perceived loss. As for myself, I do not care.

I'm blocking out any feeling of disappointment I might have, I'm blocking out any thought of what I might have won with that two grand, and I realise you can do this – you can do whatever you need to do in this situation.

It would have been unnatural not to experience some delayed reaction to the closing ceremony when I withdrew the money, after I had bombarded my brain for so many years with this winning and losing, winning and losing. And, yes, in the core of my being I can feel some ancient reflex of disappointment, but I can block it out, just block it out. I can play whatever trick I need to play on the addicted creature inside me, as long as it keeps me out of the game.

It was still necessary, I feel, to perform that ceremony, to empty the tank, to make the gesture to the gambling gods, display my indifference.

I can still feel the beautiful vibes of the meeting. I am still strong. I can still imagine the person I am in the process of becoming, a person I used to be a long time ago, a person who stood at the edge of the tide this evening, in some state of grace, let us call it that, and who had his last bet, and who then went to the right place.

Yes, let us call it a state of grace, a thing I never understood in all the years they talked about it in that church because they didn't understand it either. It doesn't have any ready meaning; it just happens to you when you move out of yourself and, for an instant, you see everything that is right and everything that is wrong.

I can still hold on to that moment of illumination. I still know how it works and how it will not work. I can keep it simple.

Here is the simple way. I will stop gambling, and I will

stay stopped. I will start some better life, somehow, and I will stay started. And if I have to go to jail, I will do it for as short a time as possible. These things are all absolutely connected, and tonight I feel I am capable of doing them all as they should be done, and of emerging glorious.

Here is another way. Ed is not wrong: there is merit in the idea – in the theory – that a large cash donation to my victims may also bring some benefit to me. No, he is not wrong. But what Ed does not understand is that I am out of the game. That I can't handle it anymore. And that I have realised I don't have to handle it anymore, that I can surrender, hand it all over, and no one will judge me for that. On the contrary, they will praise me and they will welcome me into the company of good people.

I have been powerless for a long time and I knew only the brutal side of that, the abuse I took. I fought against it, when I had nothing to fight it with, and it exhausted me. But there was another kind of powerlessness I had visited on myself, and that I could not see. At the meeting tonight they spoke of this as the first step, the acceptance that, in our addiction, we are powerless.

And when we accept that, we are not victims anymore, or perpetrators. We are independent, which is what we were always trying to be anyway when we entered the ring.

CHAPTER 16

I hear the approaching sound of Neil Young and the Stray Gators wailing loudly, then an Alfa Romeo pulls in beside me at the top of the village. Ed rolls down the window. 'Bad luck, Johnny,' he says, repeating his text to me.

I get in beside him. I inhale the smoke from his cigarette. There is a strong stench of stale smoke in the car, as there is indeed from the man himself, with cigarette butts thrown everywhere so that the vehicle seems like one enormous ashtray. I turn the Neil Young down low, not because I don't love it but because I can't keep going back there, I just can't.

'On the contrary, I feel that my luck has finally turned,' I say.

'You'll have another crack at it?' he says.

'Forget it, Ed.'

He ignores that. He still thinks I blew the money. 'I've put another two grand in there for you. You see, Johnny, any clown can get a job and make a wage. To get by without working is the gift,' he says.

I don't reply. Neil Young singing 'Out On The Weekend' is already consuming me with its raw lonesome beauty, each thump of the bass drum gently dragging me back.

'Careful,' he says, gesturing towards a couple of plastic bags at my feet, one with bottles in it, the other with ice.

I take the bag with me when we get out at the caravan, but I am determined not to drink, or to engage in any other form of degenerate behaviour tonight with Ed. Even if I wanted to, and I guess there will never be a time when I am completely free of not wanting to, on this night it would be such a betrayal, not just of my own good intentions but of the decency shown to me at the meeting, the integrity of it.

'Take that other two grand off the bookie and put it back on your credit card, like I did,' I say to Ed, laying his provisions on the counter.

'Don't give me that shit,' he says. He is teasing me rather than berating me, as if he thinks I'm just delaying the inevitable.

'I didn't lose the money. I didn't punt it. I withdrew it,' I say.

Ed is already throwing ice cubes into two glasses he's found, adding the Gordon's gin and the Schweppes tonic.

'Bullshit,' he says.

'It'll show up back on your credit card in a couple of days,' I say.

'Don't give me that shit,' he says again. It's like he thinks I'm stalling.

He holds out the glass to me, but I refuse it. 'No drink for me either,' I say.

He throws back his own. He turns away from me, still apparently relaxed. He opens the laptop and logs on to his account. 'Never had the balls that you have to put a few grand on a race. To put a few grand on anything.'

'It didn't take much balls. Half the time it wasn't even my own money.'

'I don't know how you do it,' he says, with a note of real humility. He closes the lid of the laptop respectfully.

'It's easy . . . if you have the disease,' I say.

He assumes a thoughtful face. 'I still couldn't do it. Wouldn't even dream of betting thousands the way you do. Hundreds of thousands.'

'You talk like you're some sort of a humble civil servant, instead of . . . whatever you are,' I say.

He starts the Super Ser, hunkering down in front of it, staring into the little flame, the gin and tonic on the floor beside him. 'What am I, Johnny? What do I do?' he says.

'You run a kind of a whorehouse and a drinking den down there. Down there in that lovely house where we all would meet and where your mother used to bring us mugs of tea and plates of sandwiches,' I say.

He lets out a knowing snigger, as if he's heard all that stuff before. 'I guess the kid told you that.'

'He doesn't really know. Doesn't care much either.'

'I don't do any of that other stuff. I just run a little late-night bar, for late-night people.'

'No whores, then?'

'Only the ones who are looking for a drink and some conversation at four in the morning.'

'Conversation?'

'They talk to me,' he says. He rattles his big glass of fizzy alcohol, as if reflecting on all the wise counsel he has dispensed to these girls. 'That girl who was murdered, Mary, she talked to me. She knew she was in danger. She was screwing it up for everyone.'

'Like, by sitting beside that poor bastard in Mass with his wife next to him?'

He seems surprised that I would know this.

'James,' I explain.

'Can you imagine how the guy must have felt, with all that space in the church, and her moving in beside them anyway? Can you imagine?' he says.

'And what about the girl? Maybe he'd made promises to her,' I say.

'She just wasn't cut out for it, you know? Didn't realise the stakes.' He moves away from the Super Ser, taking his drink with him. He goes to the counter and starts to tinker with the laptop.

'And the list of clients. Anyone we know?' I say.

'Anyone who is anyone.'

'You've seen the list?'

'Some of those good burghers are going to fall so far they might end up drinking in my place.'

'Part of me would love to go down there with you, Ed. But another part of me would be afraid of it . . . that's the better part.'

'Afraid?' he says, as if the thought is outlandish.

'Afraid it might break my fucking heart.'

He considers this with some respect. 'We're all a bit sentimental,' he says.

'It's more than that. I've been to a meeting tonight.'

'OK . . .'

'I'm taking that shit seriously, Ed.'

He's not fighting me about this, but he's not going away either. He takes off his leather jacket as the heat and the gin start to force little drops of sweat onto his forehead. His blotches are out tonight too, making him look horribly unhealthy, which is a comfort to me in my struggle, showing me the dissipation that awaits the transgressor.

He lowers all of his largeness onto the floor and arranges himself into a kind of a lotus position. He waves his glass at me and sighs. 'To know the nature of your own misfortune, that is the cruellest thing,' he says.

'Right,' I say.

'Guys like you, Jim Hallahan, really bright guys who are aware at every point exactly what is happening to them, the scale of it . . . it's worse for you guys, you highly sensitive types.'

'But it's worse for him than it is for me.'

I am doing that thing, making comparisons with others who are either less fortunate or more fortunate than myself, and I resolve to stop doing it from now on. I'm sure it will only hinder my recovery.

'People should feel more sympathy for you guys than for some criminal fucker who's going to spend half his life in jail anyway. But instead people take more pleasure in it. They're so glad it's not them.'

'I know that,' I say.

He takes a long drink and lights a cigarette. I join him in this, recalling that most of the people at the meeting were unembarrassed smokers.

Ed comes back with new energy. 'Why do we think we can handle life? How do we not know that life is too much for most of us? That it's just too hard?'

'There's help out there, if we ask for it.'

'Mary Tallon, the girl who got killed, it was too much for her. She couldn't just live the life she was given, accept what she had to do and stop the fucking messing.'

'She could have got out of that life – we can all get out of the life we have. Even you can do it, Ed . . . get help.'

'Help, my arse!' he shouts.

'But when it gets too much ...'

'You accommodate.'

'Accommodate?'

'You work out some ... accommodation, some way you can live in this world, some way to make it easy on yourself.' He offers me his own glass of booze, like it contains some ingredient that would bring me enlightenment.

'That's what I've been trying to do tonight, Ed. Looking for a way ...' I wave away his offer of some slightly used gin and tonic.

He drinks it himself, in one long draught, as if demonstrating all the good it's doing him. 'That way is too hard, Johnny. It's too hard,' he says.

Whether he is trying to convince me or himself I can't rightly tell. But I know this: everything he is saying is very attractive and so very dangerous for a man in my situation.

The fact that he himself is in a very poor situation, sick in body and in soul, does not diminish the weight of his argument. Life is too much for most of us, too hard, and we get into too much trouble, and the way out of that trouble is maybe even harder.

But I fight off that thought, like a bluesman jousting with the devil. I fight it off by thinking about the text James sent me, seeing Ed not as some demonic voice putting all these bad ideas into my head but as a man who has tried to help me, just as the guys in the meeting tried to help me. In fact,

Ed has helped me more. He has shown me what it looks like if you keep going down.

So I will try to help him. That's what I will do. And already that thought is making me feel lighter, releasing the tension. When I first saw that text coming in from James, *The best way to help yourself is to help other people*, I felt it was a fine sentiment, a bit like my own when I wanted to go to Africa, but one that was probably coming from a young man with a bit of therapy behind him, who hadn't had all those feel-good lines kicked out of him by life.

Now, as I look at Ed oozing gin and tonic and perspiration, a man who has reached the bottom just as surely as I did myself, I see again all the beauty of James's idea. I see how those who commit themselves to helping others really are freer than the rest of us, free of self-absorption, free of guilt.

'We can help each other here,' I say.

'Fuck off with that stuff. I'm in no need of help,' he says.

'You've already helped me in a lot of ways.'

He takes a long drink. He hangs his head in contemplation. 'I am not one to judge,' he says. He unravels himself from the lotus position. His body has stiffened up. He tries some stretching exercises, leaning forward, as if he is praying to Mecca, then settling back on his heels.

'James says there's an outside chance of a suspended sentence, all of it suspended. An outside chance,' I say.

'Fuck,' he says quietly. He sighs, as if he'll never find the one position in which he can be comfortable.

'They're looking more kindly on the likes of me these days. Addicts, you know?'

He shuts his eyes and winces as if struck by a headache. 'If James says that, then James is maybe not the best lawyer of all time.'

'You think?'

'I'm not dissing him, I'm just . . .'

'He didn't say I'd get off, only that we'd give it a shot.'

'If I was defending you . . .'

'Jesus . . .'

'If I was defending you, I wouldn't raise your hopes like that unless I was a hundred per cent sure.'

'If you were defending me, I'd have no hope anyway.'

Ed just can't find a position in which he's at ease. He stretches out on the floor, then thinks better of it, gets up and heads down to the long seat to stretch out on it. He holds his drink against his chest as he speaks. 'You know he went to that Al-Anon shit?'

'Yes.'

'So he could reflect on what a terrible man I am.'

'It's not about you, Ed.'

'I hate all that shit. I really, really hate it. I hate the AA and I hate the GA and the NA and I hate counsellors and every other bunch of fucks with their Twelve Steps and their Higher Power and their cups of tea and their Marietta fucking biscuits.'

'You don't think that as a result of that shit James is maybe in a better place than, eh, some other people?'

'James . . . he's looked into that addiction business a bit too much, sees it everywhere.'

'He could be right.'

'Thinks everyone he sees is deeply damaged.'

'Am I not deeply damaged? Is that not what brought me down?'

He gives himself a little time to make a measured response. 'That could be the reason . . . that could be it all right. It could be something deep inside you . . . or . . . it could just be that you backed the wrong fucking horses.'

He lets out a snort, the sound of dissipation. He rolls off the long seat and wanders up for another drink. He seems to begrudge all the effort he is making to get there. Maybe he is begrudging me my few hours of sobriety.

'Right,' I say.

'You know what my mother used to say about you? That you had lovely manners.'

'I liked her,' I say.

He fills his glass messily with ice, gin and tonic, making me feel unmannerly that I am not doing it for him. 'You had lovely manners. Maybe you had a lovely manner about you . . . she liked the way you made cups of tea and handed them around to everyone, even though you didn't have to.'

It may be the only good thing that people say about me when I'm dead, that at least I had manners. I've heard it before from others. I'm getting tired of it. 'Anything else?'

He takes a while over this. 'She'd laugh at you saying the wrong thing at the wrong time.'

'Right.'

He takes a long drink, knocking back the gin and tonic as if it was lemonade on a hot day. 'She would have been disgusted to see how you've turned out.'

I am thinking she would not have been overly pleased to see her house turned into some sort of shebeen by her cherished son, who now styles himself a happy alcoholic, but I also seem to be drifting towards another dimension in which I forget that I will soon be standing up in a courtroom, possibly – indeed, probably – listening to a judge sentencing me to a few years in prison, and adding a few lines of condemnation of his own. Drifting towards a dimension in which I forget that the case will probably be reported in every paper in this country and a few others, that I will be seen on the main evening news walking into the courthouse, with a bunch of journalists all over me. I can't block out those visions anymore. I am only surprised that I have beaten them away from time to time, and that even with just a few days to go, I have found this new power that is taking some of the weight off me. By all conventional measurements I have never been in such a terrible situation, and I am starting to wonder if this happens to other people, if there is some fundamental energy that always rises up at such times, some anaesthetic hidden inside us, which emerges only when we are in most desperate need.

Still, I know the right thing to do. This in itself is a beautiful idea, to be able to see beyond misfortune and circumstance, to have this clarity.

The right thing to do, in this case, involves doing very little, which is also an attraction. Little more than keeping it simple. Which in my case, at this time, consists merely of staying out of Ed's online account, and all the wonders and terrors that await me therein.

I know the right thing to do because of these two meetings, with James and with the recovering gamblers, Paul and the other guys, whose names I've already forgotten. It is they who have given me this direction, who have somehow appeared in my life with these blessings. It is the third meeting, with Ed, that is testing me.

I know that if I get myself right in the head, I may yet have a life. Even though I will be in jail, I may yet have a life. And, still, Ed is right: life is too much, it is too hard. It's too hard for him, it is hard enough for young James and it is hard for me.

And there's something else that Ed is right about. I can continue to gamble all the way to the gates of the penitentiary, and nobody will know a thing about it, apart from me and Ed and his bookmaker.

I could not do that if my disease involved drinking or drugging or eating or sex, but with this thing I have, there is a magnificent silence all the way down to the bottom. Yes, we may roar in anguish when we know that we are alone and unheard, but until they're actually breaking down the door with a sledgehammer, we can enjoy a state of great secrecy.

Until all the money is gone, all the money we won, all the money we could borrow or steal, all the folding money and all the plastic money, until that moment arrives and we can't hide it anymore, until then we can get dressed and we can go to work and we can display all the calm of a man with no problems, a man with the most excellent manners, even when everyone else is feeling the strains of the day. As we try to contain a thousand terrifying propositions in our heads, we can seem like friendly fellows, like contented fools.

So, yes, Ed is not wrong about this, as he is not wrong about many things. And still I know the right thing to do. I know it perfectly well.

I just don't know if I can do it.

CHAPTER 17

Tonight the drink and the talk are taking the energy out of him. It's hardly even eleven o'clock and Ed is making noises about leaving, just like anyone would. It feels like I have triumphed over him in some way, that by introducing these ideas of redemption and rehabilitation I have quietened him. Or maybe, as he might assess it himself, I am just not on his wavelength due to my lack of drink. He did not necessarily start his day's drinking when he arrived at the caravan – in fact, it is most unlikely that he got as far as the late evening without soaking up a few litres of the old Winston Smith along the way.

He is gathering himself to leave, in a ponderous fashion,

and in this high place that I have found for myself, I can even glimpse a man who is considering his position in relation to his own disease.

But he does not talk about such things. He is leaving me with what he regards as a gift. He puts a bundle of cash on the counter, a load of notes wrapped in an elastic band. 'You must have this money,' he says.

'No, thanks,' I say.

'Just check into a hotel for a few days.'

'Couldn't stand that, Ed. Couldn't stand having to exchange a nice hotel room for a prison cell.'

'Take it anyway.' He shrugs.

I figure there's about a thousand there. 'Money never brought me anything but grief,' I say.

Ed looks around the caravan with a doleful expression. Through his eyes I can see even more clearly that it's like some kind of coffin for the undead. 'Poverty didn't bring you much either, Johnny.'

I want to reply that it only brought me to a land beyond my wildest dreams, and that was just today, but he would clearly regard that merely as GA jargon that will soon fade away. 'Will you mind that money for me, if I go down?' I say.

'Of course. I'll invest it for you.'

I guide him to the door and out to his car. Even with a barrel-load of booze on board, he probably knows the way home, where he will wait for the night people to arrive. He turns the key in the ignition and the CD player starts up loud, the voice of Neil Young taking us all the way back to the beginning.

'That stuff has destroyed us too,' I say.

'Neil Young?'

'The lot of it.'

Ed lowers the volume, as if something has occurred to him, and the music is distracting him. He looks straight ahead, apparently trying to make out something in the distance. He starts talking, as if there's nobody else there, not addressing his words to me . . .

'It was Neil Young, "Out On The Weekend", not "Linden Arden". It was Neil Young,' he says.

'What?' I say.

'That night at the party, you and Annie. "Out On The Weekend" was the song that was playing, the *Harvest* album. Not "Linden Arden", like I said. "Out On The Weekend" . . .'

'Ah, Jesus,' I say, the truth of it landing on me, landing hard.

Ed stops it there, still not looking at me. It seems to be landing on him too, remembering this thing that happened, or that might have happened. Yes, even the thought that it might have happened is hard to take. 'That's the one,' he says.

'Ah, Jesus,' I say again, as the song resonates in some long-dormant part of my subconscious. I am remembering the shape of it, the possibility of it. Now I remember sitting there with Annie, I do remember that song.

'You know what you do now? You say, "Fuck it . . . Fuck it,"
and forget it,' he says.

'"Out On The Weekend",' I say, listening to it turned down
low in Ed's car, hearing it at a party a thousand years ago.

Ed is looking at me now, grabbing my arm. 'That's what
you do now. You say, "Fuck it," and forget it,' he says, like
some famously successful person imparting their most
precious secret.

'Sure, Ed,' I say, all the fine thoughts of the fellowship
starting to drain out of me as I contemplate another defeat,
one that I didn't see coming.

He lets go of my arm and starts the car. He turns the music
back up. It's on the second track of the album now, 'Harvest'
itself. 'On the upside, Neil changed his direction after this
record and I think both of us enjoyed the darker material
that followed,' he says.

He drives away, the music trailing behind him, without
knowing if my response is to break a bottle of gin over his
head or to burst out laughing. I can see the merit in both,
about equally, and I guess that's how he gets away with it. I
guess it's a weakness in me too, another one.

Back in the caravan I boil a kettle for some tea, just to
be doing something, but it's only making me angry that I
didn't ask Ed to leave me some of his Gordon's, that I didn't
even take the one he offered me. I sit at the counter drinking
the tea: such a restlessness has come over me that I think I
might walk up and down the caravan all night if I don't sit

there with all my determination. I am wondering if a swift gin and tonic would put me right, but all I have is tea. And I am running out of cigarettes.

The restlessness will not go away, because now I remember I never even said thank you to Ed for the money, even with all my manners, and I think I should ring him now to put that right: thanks for the two grand he put into the account and thanks for the thousand sitting there, maybe his way of saying there may be something left for me at the end of this shit-rain. And thanks for clearing up a few things for me – I understand now, completely, what he meant when he was wanting to call me an eejit the other night: he was trying to get it across to me that I'm not just a smart guy who has these odd lapses into immaturity, which is how I was seeing it, but that there is something in me that is so self-defeating it is virtually a form of madness, a strain of incapability running right through me, that will always do me down.

Ed knows these things, and I have been pushing him back. He has always known what is good for me, and what is wrong with me, when I couldn't see it myself. He saw it most startlingly on the night when Annie gave me the signal, and I didn't see it. I didn't get it.

And I don't even know for sure if Ed is right. I don't even know if what he saw, or what he thinks he saw, or what he heard from some other happy drunkard is what actually happened with Annie and me. Our brains are all messed up. We don't remember things as they were, we didn't even know what was happening at the time, or didn't want to know – but now I remember sitting there with Annie, I do remember that song. The way I had worked it out, it was that night at the cinema with the snow on the ground when it went wrong. It was partly my fault and partly Annie's fault. I had worked it out like that with good reason – I did not want to feel what I am feeling now.

But it's here anyway.

The way Ed saw it, that night in his house, it was not partly my fault and partly her fault, it was all me. And I concede that he may be right, that I let this get away from me because I just wasn't paying attention, or because of the beer, or the music, but mainly because of the way I am. Because I was born to the people I was born to, because of the way we were, and the way that we lived. Because of everything that made me feel I was no good. And because I was afraid.

We are afraid of everything in the world, we addicts – we are afraid of crossing the road.

But we all get a bit of luck, and the way I see it now, Annie was my luck. I thought for a while that winning my little house in the Coombe was my luck, the one big stroke that I needed, but it wasn't really. Annie was my luck, and it got away from me that night. So I have become Mr Masarella but the other way round: he had a stroke of great good fortune that he never knew about; with me it was this moment of misfortune.

Down all the years, I ran a different version of it in my head. I rationalised it and minimised it in so many ways but, Christ, it was a terrible mistake. And now that it's all moved from my brain to my gut, I can feel this sadness hitting me so hard, it's like I have been winded, like the day I was attacked by Christina, except I'd felt that one coming for a long time; in some odd way I was ready.

I was not ready for this.

I am going to ring Ed to ask him to come back here to drink with me, when I get a different urge, strong enough at least to make me stand up straight.

I log on to his betting account, a thoughtless reflex just to see what is happening in the world. It really does make me feel a bit less lonesome to gaze on all these possibilities, to see that there is American football going on at this moment, near midnight, and that in theory I can get involved. I'm sure that after a few hundred more meetings of Gamblers Anonymous I will arrive at a broader understanding of this, of how I dealt with feelings of sadness and isolation not by connecting with other people but by attaching myself to games and events such as this, to occasions that otherwise have nothing to do with me, whose players do not know or care that I exist.

After five hundred meetings I may see myself very clearly as someone who could have had a proper life with real relationships and children and all that human chaos, instead of hitching a ride on this train of fools. And getting the chaos anyway, the worst kind, the kind that empties the spirit.

But I don't know if I'll even make it to the next meeting, which is the only one that matters.

There is some unbroken part of me that is urging me to try to sleep, maybe not in the damp bedroom tonight but there on the window seat with the heater going. To try to sleep because I am exhausted, and also because it will stop me thinking about this tennis match in Rio de Janeiro that has just started.

There are a few things drawing me to this tennis match, the first of which is just that it's on, at present, and there are about a hundred different betting options, so many ways to get involved. And there is also this feeling of mortification that I devoted the best years of my life to such low-class entertainment, to tennis matches in Rio, and have wandered so long in this idiot's paradise.

Yes, I can still just go to sleep, and do nothing, but these are such days I will probably not sleep, no matter how tired I am.

I am so tired, but I will sleep soon, that ordinary sleep. I know another kind: I have heard it said that, after a night of gambling at the roulette wheel in one of those upper-class London casinos of the 1970s, a night during which some aristocrat eventually lost a stately home and a few thousand acres, that loser emerged into the morning with a light step and an air of vitality, as if he had slept. I always remembered that line, because I knew it was right – 'It was as if he had slept.'

That is the kind of rest the gambler is looking for, maybe the kind I am looking for tonight, as I start to follow this no-mark tennis match in Rio, thinking that there was a time when I would have punted twenty grand on it, just to pass the time.

I know nothing about this particular match, but I can see it in the mind's eye, this event with about seven spectators watching it, and about seven hundred thousand punters watching the points racking up on their internet scoreboards. I know enough about tennis to understand how this one seems to be going. If the favourite had woken up with a sore neck or was otherwise having an off day, or maybe if there was something a little dubious going down in those South American markets, we would see it reflected in the score by now. But the favourite is playing exactly as the favourite should, and already the other player is an outsider at odds of 10/1, and drifting. The players have names other than 'the favourite' and 'the outsider', but I do not care enough to let them settle in my brain; I would not waste my time.

When the first set finishes in an untroubled 6–2 and the price of the outsider settles at 12/1, I have an urge to put Ed's two grand on at that price, €2,000 to win €24,000. It is a mug's bet, a bad gambler's play, and still I have the urge. I have seen so many of these low-level matches change so fast: just a few stray points can bring about a momentum swing, and the odds on your hopeless outsider are suddenly tumbling. A few hours ago I would have felt utterly estranged from this game, as if I had gone through a door, closed it softly behind me and was standing outside my old world. Not in some figurative sense, but physically standing there, on the other side. And behind that door there was all the filth of that doomed existence, all closed down now.

Now I am right back in there, with my finger on the button: 'Bet Now'.

I have not pressed the button, but my finger is resting on it, and I have typed the number 2000 into the slot. I could turn that into a proper stake very quickly, a five-figure number, and the fact that I am making such calculations at all tells me that I am already seeing this as the smart play, the play that no power can deny me. They told me at the meeting about my Higher Power, but now there is a power in my world that is even higher than that, the power of that number, the weight of it crushing everything else, the energy of it racing through my blood. And I can feel this grief and this anger rising again in me, anger that my life has been devoured by these three-card-trick merchants, anger that I have no gin to drink, that I am running out of cigarettes, and that I am running out of days.

But still I have this tremendous need to place that bet, still I want to press that key. I think that I am losing my mind and I know there is no way out of this.

The favourite drops serve in the first game of the next set. I see the outsider coming down to six to one. I feel that momentum swinging. I press the button: 'Bet Now'.

It is done. I am hooked up to the old machine at dead of night. I am involved again. And I am winning. The outsider is sweeping through the second set. I am hoping that the favourite has picked up an injury and has too much character just to retire, that she will keep on struggling through the third set until I can collect.

I can feel those beautiful endorphins starting up in me again – maybe that is the only cure for a grief like mine. My player has won the second set. It's an even-money game now. I have a serious prospect of winning twelve grand on this, punting that on the next event that catches my attention, and on into infinity. And it gives me a feeling of pride. Which, after the other feelings I've been through this evening, is an anaesthetic.

Twelve grand . . . plus my stake of two grand is fourteen grand and I'm going to win this now. I am already looking through the matches that are about to start, looking to reinvest.

There's a match on another court in Rio, between two women who seem to be of similar ability. The odds are just a shade below evens for both of them: 10/11, it is like the toss of a coin. I wait for the number 14,000 to land in Ed's account, and I put it all on the player on the right-hand side as I look at the screen, it's as thoughtless as that, and yet not unwise, because who, after all, gives much thought to whether they are calling heads or tails? It is just an instinct, and for me, tonight, it is looking like a fine instinct, because this game is running perfectly almost from the first ball.

I am starting to feel the joy again of my old profession. I am remembering how good I used to be, and how good it made me feel to be ahead, to be miles ahead. And while it will take me a long time to get to that place again, I am getting a shaft of optimism that, by the end of this night, I will at least be a lot less behind than I have been.

I am going to win this second bet, easily, and then I am going to consolidate. I am scanning the markets for a clear favourite, for some free money. I find a candidate. I put all that I have, nearly twenty-seven grand, on a player whose name I recognise, quite a high-ranking player, as I recall, which is why she will probably do this for me quite handily at odds of 1/4, raising me up to over thirty-three thousand for the evening, and to a place where I am not feeling much pain, not much pain at all. I have somehow hit this vein of form and I can feel it staying with me for another few hours, maybe for another twenty-four hours. At this moment I can see myself grinding until I am in a position to take a figure adjacent to five hundred grand into that courtroom, just to get the blood flowing.

It is looking indeed like the free money I thought it would be, with my selection racing through the first set, 6–2. It's looking like thirty-three thousand, no problem. Then the game turns . . .

It is a bastard of a game, tennis, and I would never watch it for pleasure. But it has an ingenious scoring system, which means that a point taken or lost at a certain time can change everything. Which is an inspiration to the gambler, as is the fact that there are no draws.

There's just a winner and a loser, and when these things are running in your favour, it leaves you incandescent with the love of life. And when they're running against you, as is happening to me now, it drags every good thing out of you. It empties you.

This game is turning the wrong way. My one is down 2–0 in the third set. I am looking abjectly at the points racking up against her with not much racking up against the other side. I can feel that this bet is going down. It is going down without a doubt.

I close the lid of the laptop and raise it high above my head. I am about to bring it down on the counter with such a smash, until I remember that I still have about two hundred euro left in my own account, not the gambling account, the account I was living off, the only money I have left in the world. But then I see Ed's bundle of cash and I'm free of that little confusion.

My hands are shaking now with anger and with shame, with all that glorious adrenalin gone bad inside me, turned to acid. I am in my own account now, looking at a baseball game, which is nearly over but may yield a quick return and get me rolling again. The teams are level. I put the two hundred on Chicago at slightly worse than evens, hoping to get nearly four hundred back, and on and on until I am flying.

That bet goes down too, and now I really have nothing in

there, I am bereft. I am mad now, not just mad with anger, mad in the other way too, crazy mad. I do not bother this time with the bourgeois nicety of closing the lid on the machine, I just raise it over my head and start smashing it off the counter as hard as I can, so hard that it seems strange to me that the counter does not break. I smash it again, three times, four times, and the laptop breaks asunder. This box, which had inveigled me into its labyrinth so many times, is now battered into a heap of trash.

I step over the remains of the machine. I drag my duvet and a pillow out of the bedroom and down to the seat at the window. As I take off my clothes I fold them carefully, almost in a spirit of self-parody. I am trying to quieten the madness inside me, the rage, the self-hatred and the total disgust that I had let myself go again, that I could be visited by the old compulsion on such a night, so unexpectedly.

I am nauseous, about three-quarters of the way to vomiting, and still I am thinking about what might be going on down there on some clay court in Rio, because it hits me that I could just call Ed, and ask him to stick another two grand into the account – which would work, if I hadn't made the amateur error of destroying the machine. And if I had another bet, on another laptop, I could be sitting up again following every point, perhaps in the end to be destroyed one more time at the sight of the empty account, to marvel at how my endeavours could have turned to absolute zero, just by dint of a wrong call on a matter of no importance, the two noughts before the decimal point and the two noughts after it, everything gone. Or maybe to look at ten thousand or twenty thousand euro, yes, maybe that.

But even I, hollowed out as I am, fool that I most certainly am, even I can take some wisdom out of what I have done. I did smash that machine. I did what was necessary. That is what it took to stop me having another bet tonight. That is what it may take some other day. That is how bad I've got it.

I should probably be feeling some ordinary human concern at the waste of a decent machine, but looking at it there, all busted on the floor, I do not feel that concern. No, I do not give a fuck.

When I wake I feel better than I usually feel. Usually I have this sense of emptiness, which is the best part, like a man with cancer who is not aware of his condition until it creeps back into his consciousness after these few moments in neutral. Today the emptiness is followed by recollections of the previous day with Ed, then with James and with the people of the fellowship. And then I remember the music in Ed's car and the moment of realisation about Annie and what it did to me, how it cut me up, and then the betting, the betting . . . I can see the remains of all that on the floor.

By now I would usually be remembering that I am still probably going to jail, that those moments of quietness were just a trick of the mind, a reminder of the time before

I had this disease, and a premonition of the time after, when there will be nothing at all. By now I would be down.

But instead I am visited by a different energy, a realisation that it is wrong to see this as a cancer. It is intellectually and morally wrong because I have a cure for this thing within myself. I just couldn't see it. Or maybe I didn't have the heart for it.

I didn't have the heart, and maybe this was what got me in the end. I wonder: who was the first man to think of that term and realise that he didn't have the heart, the courage, whatever you call it? Yes, the courage is better: it is the most admirable thing of all, courage, and I am in awe of it when I see it in others, but it seems that I did not possess it. Not the right kind anyway.

The kind that I have is the kind that allowed me to turn on the machine and to punt thousands in the middle of the night on a tennis match in South America, but I did not have the better kind that would enable me to turn off the machine, and stop.

CHAPTER 18

I get a meeting a day, for eight days, in the village, in the town and outside the town. What happened to me was a slip, according to James, a term I am not familiar with in that way, but one they use in the fellowships to describe what happens when somebody breaks out and does the dog on it. A slip – I like it, I must say. It has a lovely understatement. And it seems that you can just go back to the meetings and start again, which is very attractive to the gambler, who has spent so much of his career starting again, and again, who craves the clean slate.

James brings me to the meetings and he waits for me and then he brings me home. He refrains from judging me, because he is wise, and maybe because that verdict has been in for a long time. He takes me to the town to see the addiction counsellor, himself a recovering gambler, who has no trouble believing that I am serious when I say I have finally had enough. I don't tell either of them about these visions of Annie, because I just can't do it. I am afraid of what happens when I go back there.

In these days I receive no calls or visits from Ed, who has doubtless seen the activity in his betting account. I imagine him looking at all those zeroes in the top corner, as I have often looked at them myself, realising that our debate is over, that there's no arguing with a zero.

Now it is the day before we go to court and the way I see this now, it is an each-way bet. If we can convince the judge that I am sincerely in recovery and may be of more service to the community outside jail than inside, that would be a result. And if they send me down anyway, the fact that I am getting out of this game and that I am never going back in – or at least not today – is also a result.

But even thinking about it in those terms feels wrong to me. I am hungry now for the fellowship, high on this new thing like any beginner.

But I am cold too, in this caravan that was not meant for winter, cold even though I have slept in my clothes, something I had managed to avoid doing even in this penitentiary. After contemplating the state of my spirit, I am brought down to the question of whether I am too cold to take my clothes off and have a shower, or whether the heat of the water will make it seem worthwhile. Or whether I can stand another shower anyway in that cubicle, which is too small for me and makes me long for the showers that Christina and I used to have in one of the several bathrooms in our old place, all that opulence.

Then I see Ed's bundle of cash on the counter, and I realise I can still get a little of that opulence back tonight. I can do as he says and check into a hotel in the town, maybe the Central, which used to have a big ballroom, where we would go on Saturday nights to a disco, really to drink.

I like the thought of it, the warm, clean hotel room, but I can't quite commit to it. This place is disgusting but it is still mine. It is, in fact, the only thing left in the world that is mine. Now that the laptop lies there in smithereens, I own nothing except the clothes I slept in and the clothes that are squashed into the wardrobe, the Super Ser, the cylinder of gas that is running it, and the cylinder out the back.

It is not much, to be sure, but it still gives me the illusion that there is some small part of this world in which I am the person in charge. To move on to a hotel room would make me feel that I am handing over that illusion for clean sheets, a full Irish breakfast and Sky News – which I may well be getting in prison anyway.

And regardless of what James has been saying, and what I have been thinking, I am not letting myself get too attached to the hope that I will not be going to prison. I have been in the hoping game far too long for that.

Instead I am comforting myself with a more manageable hope: the prospect of an open prison, like the one I saw pictured in the paper a few years ago, a bit like a suburban housing estate somewhere in the midlands. I recall a line about the prisoners being able to order a Chinese takeaway on a Friday night.

But I am cold now, too cold for a shower, I decide. I have a number for a local taxi company on a card I picked up in the chipper, thinking I might book him for my journey tomorrow to the courthouse – these are the things I must think about now.

There is another meeting this evening in a hall a few miles away from the village. I will get a taxi there. And this morning I just like the idea of getting a taxi somewhere and paying for it out of Ed's bundle of notes, a sense of luxurious indulgence that may be related to my own period as a taxi driver – wherever it takes me, as long as it is warmer than this place, will be fine.

I calculate roughly from the cash bundle that I could in theory strike a deal with the taxi driver for him to spend the day driving me all around the country for one last look at everything. But I think I'll just get him to take me into the town, to meet James as arranged, like a responsible person.

Something about that bundle on the counter reminds me of betting too, as a scenario forms in my mind of the taxi driver pulling in outside a bookmaker's office on the way into the town, stopping the meter and saying he'll be back in a minute, he just needs to have a few quid on something. And when he's been gone for ten minutes, fifteen minutes, I get impatient and I follow him in there – I am angry, not because he's been delayed but because I'm assuming he regards me with such contempt that he feels fine about me sitting out there. With the tiny amount of self-respect that going to GA and smashing the laptop has given me, I am going to confront him, but when I get in there I back down.

In a welter of apologies he indicates that he's had a winner and he's going again on the next race, and maybe I should consider having a few quid on it too. I am back in a betting office again, in the company of down-going men, losing myself in that atmosphere raddled with hope and desperation and misfortune, intoxicated by it. Seized by the old compulsion I peel off a few fifties from Ed's bundle – it's what he would have wanted. I scribble down the name of the taximan's horse on the docket with a betting-office biro, write five hundred euro next to it, and push it across the counter just before the start of the race, some no-mark all-weather event at Musselburgh. I watch the race with the fever surging through me again, that primal need for a winner, that feeling of utter emptiness when it's a loser. A monkey gone and a monkey left. Maddened now that I have succumbed again I start chasing, lumping the rest of the money on the favourite in the next race, and again it's bet-down. In the mind's eye I see myself getting into some dispute with the taxi driver, something about him wanting to leave now, and me wanting to stay. I see a fight, more punters getting involved, I see the guards arriving, and in the end I see myself having to call James from the garda station to tell him that our defence strategy no longer exists. Indeed, far from sending me forth to give talks in schools about the gambling phenomenon, the judge might even be throwing in a few extra months for causing an affray.

It is not a bad thing, I reason, for this to be happening in my imagination. It shows that I am being vigilant, that I am anticipating the unexpected, the way that a person's life can change in a few seconds of agitation.

And still, as I put that well-wrapped bundle into my coat pocket, it doesn't feel like money at all. It just feels like betting money.

CHAPTER 19

I think it was called Henry's. It's called Romany now, and it's a coffee place, not a pub as Henry's used to be, a pub with a three-piece band at the weekend.

As I confirm the arrangement over the phone with James, I can hear in my head the rumbling of the band I used to hear when I was walking past that place. I can hear a voice coming through an echo chamber to the street outside, singing 'Bad Moon Rising'.

I can talk to James now about many things, but there is so much that I cannot talk to him about, like that memory of a band playing a song on some night before he was born, not even the song itself, just the vibration of it coming down the street. And what that does to me, what it touches, a sense that everything was ahead of us then, that we were living intensely, Ed and I, that we had ambitions and not just addictions.

I do not want to talk to the taximan about anything, and I feel blessed that he turns out to be from Central or Eastern Europe, that he may not know about my situation. I see from his identification card that he is called Tony, which doesn't seem entirely right, though the picture does resemble the man who is driving. He is a neatly bearded man with glasses, probably in his thirties, wearing a shirt and tie and a waistcoat, and reminding me in some madly distorted way of one of the musicians in Hot Chocolate, who has just popped back to the present day to do a bit of taxi-driving. It is a good car he is driving too, a Lexus like the one I used to drive to and from the airport, and which for a while was my home – the gods, it seems, are still using me for their entertainment.

I sit in the back seat, to maintain that distance, to keep myself to myself, and by his friendliness I take it that the driver is happy to keep himself to himself, to think of things that are known and meaningful only to him – perhaps when I was loving bar bands and 'Bad Moon Rising' he was being born in Serbia, orphaned by the age of two.

His inner life or any other part of his life is unknown to me, but I do know that somehow he has arrived at this moment in both of our stories, and he is doing better than

I am. He may be driving a taxi, as I once did, but he has no meeting today with his solicitor, no case to construct; he has no public disgrace to endure.

Whatever weaknesses he has, whatever addictions or obsessions, they are not the kind that have you pleading with a judge for three years in jail rather than seven, and have you dreaming the impossible dream of a suspended sentence.

So, I don't feel bad or selfish about withdrawing into myself, looking out the back window at these places of my youth to which I am returning in defeat.

I look to the sea and the mountains on our right because they seem universal to me, distracting me from the specifics of the houses on my left, each one known to me and each one liable to trigger some obscure feeling of regret. I walked down this road so often going to Ed's house, coming home from it late at night. If I didn't guard against it, I might spend some time wondering how many of the people to whom I used to deliver the post along this road are still alive. Or maybe I would see some fragile old lady standing at her door, and by some feat of deduction I would see her as she used to be, a woman in her late thirties with four children charging around the place, and her at the centre of all that energy, but now inhabiting this broken-down body from which all energy is gone. No, I keep looking to the sea and the mountains.

We are passing Ed's house now, and I get this ancient urge to tell the driver to stop, that I must go in here. But I contain that urge. I get a look at that fine house, a glimpse that tells me it is still fine, and large, but I see too that the grass outside is growing high. It is so high, it could not be cut with any normal mower. You would have to get some heavy-duty cutting machine to tackle it. So if you lived there maybe you could forgive yourself if you never got around to it, if it got away from you towards the end of one summer, and after that it was too late.

I make a signal to the driver that I would like to smoke, taking out the packet and holding up a cigarette. I am guessing that an easterner who was orphaned by the age of two wouldn't give a monkey's about people smoking in his cab, and I am right. He shrugs in acceptance, and he refuses nicely when I offer him one, and as I light up, and inhale, I feel another little hit of freedom in the knowledge that I really wouldn't have cared if he had refused. I would not have felt uncomfortable. I do not give a damn what he thinks about me in any way. I am beyond such petty considerations. I am cool.

Yes, I think it was called Henry's but it's called Romany now. All the way in I'm looking at shops and pubs and cafés that are called something else now, each one challenging me to remember it as it was, like an archaeologist straining to reimagine some lost city.

The driver stops outside Romany, in the main street. With a keep-the-change gesture I give him a fifty, which I peel off the bundle in my pocket, not ostentatiously. He does not know that I have only fifties. He gives me a thank-you of real warmth, a note of appreciation in it, which tells me that indeed he knows who I am, or was told who I am. He knows who I am, and what I have done, and what I have failed to do.

I see James sitting in the window seat of Romany, a position that seems unsafe to me.

He stands up to shake hands, as if he wants everyone outside and everyone inside to see it. It's like he's read a book about positive body language, about visualisation, acting like I'm already a free man and there's no reason to hide. This coffee place is full, overcrowded with people who have come in from the cold of the afternoon, who are pretending not to stare at me, at us, and James is greeting me like I am a valued associate.

But it is still making me anxious, this feeling of exposure, of being out among people again.

He goes to the self-service counter for two bowls of tomato soup, apologising for his largeness as he squeezes between the tables.

'I have a really strong sense that the fellowship will work for you. It works for creative people,' he says.

'It works and then it doesn't work,' I say, going back over the slip, the smashing of the laptop, describing the purity of the compulsion, the unstoppability of it, the trauma of it. James urges me to start on the tomato soup. He suggests I may be in delayed shock. He offers to drive me to a meeting tonight, in Castletown.

'Ed would like me to go to a hotel and debauch myself with gambling and women,' I say.

'That's not what he wants.'

'He gave me the money for it,' I say.

'What he wants, it's clear to me . . . what he wants is you. He wants *your* company. He wants you to be his friend again . . . That's what he wants.'

He may not be wrong, but I am just slightly resenting the fact that I am taking so much instruction from someone so young. 'Maybe what he wants is your company,' I say.

'I think you're the only person he has any respect for,' he says.

'It's love, James. We love each other.'

James seems tremendously pleased by this, perhaps feeling that my move towards the fellowship has enabled me to speak openly about such things. He urges me to finish the soup. We concentrate on that for a while, then James continues, in a low voice, 'The way he tried to keep you gambling . . . Jesus . . .' he says, though he can somehow say it in a way that doesn't sound judgemental.

'I understand it, though, coming from him.'

'He didn't want you to change?'

'It's what he believes in. I think he really and truly believes that all this stuff about addiction and recovery and counselling and AA and GA and basically men doing things they don't want to do, and giving up things, is a complete crock of shit. He thinks it's wrong, and that somebody has to stand against it. Maybe he's right.'

'Maybe he's just afraid. If you can stop gambling, it puts it up to him, with his drinking,' he says, again with no harshness.

'But maybe he's right,' I say.

We go to James's office, which is situated in a side street near the courthouse. The afternoon light is dying, but the anxiety has not left me, that feeling of being visible to all, of being open to attack by anyone who fancies it. I am glad to be going with James to an office in which there will be just the two of us, yet I am still disturbed by my own vulnerability. I do not want to think of how powerless I will feel in the courtroom, or wherever I may be going after that. James wants to run through everything one more time, to settle his nerves too. We have to climb a lot of stairs to get to the office, in a building that feels about two hundred years old, in which everything seems to be very brown.

'Can I smoke?' I say.

'Sure,' James says, directing me towards an old-fashioned brown chair and pushing a cup towards me, with some cold tea in the bottom, for an ashtray.

He picks through my file, while I smoke. I figure that my mobile home is a slightly pleasanter place to be than his office, more contemporary. The courthouse, which can be seen clearly from the heights of James's office, looks older still, with its classical columns, its ridiculous grandeur.

They have captured me, all right, these old institutions,

which were around for a long time before I arrived with my fine notions, these people with their Gilbert and Sullivan evenings who would laugh in my face if I told them that Van Morrison was the greatest artist of any kind to come from this island. I would be right about that too, but they would not know it. Yet when I was embarking on my road to freedom, my gambling, they already knew all the ways that I could fall, and what might happen to me when they found out about it. It is they who will define my freedom now. It is they who will tell me what I am allowed to do, where I am allowed to go, what I can read, what I can listen to, whether I can speak.

I think again of that scene I played in my head, of the taxi driver stopping outside the betting office and me coming in after him. Oh, how they would love that to happen. How they would love to see me fall for the last time, to leave me with no defence of any kind, to give me the seven years and then to move on to the next loser and to the one after that, these creatures who are possessed of such self-regard, and I can say this because I know them well.

I was never short of clients from the law business. I made money for a lot of them, and they never asked me too many questions.

But they have me now, under the gun, and I would do well not to give them anymore ammunition. I touch the bundle of notes in my pocket, for luck.

'We have an expert who will confirm that gambling is an

addiction. It is now officially defined by the United Nations as a disease,' James says.

'Long time coming,' I drawl.

'In summary . . . first of all, we're not going to waste anybody's time so we're pleading guilty, as guilty as hell.'

'Already they like us.'

'We will describe your entry into Gamblers Anonymous, your total acceptance of your addiction and of any help such as counselling that may be required to cope with it, and to help others cope with all the damage you have done. I think we can say with some justification that you're having a kind of a spiritual awakening.'

I wave that one through.

'And we will describe your determination to give something back in the only way open to you, by offering counsel to others, by explaining the nature of your addiction in the media, by giving talks in schools and so on . . . Essentially we're saying that you're worth far more to society outside jail than inside.'

'But I'm still the Ponzi Man, so seven years . . .'

'Your sincerity will shine through, I'm sure of that. They'll know if you're really in recovery or if you're just trying it on.'

'They . . . the judge . . .'

'You'd be surprised at how many people stay out of jail,' he says.

I flick some ash into the cup, enjoying the hiss as it meets the cold tea. I wave that one through too.

Then James searches for something on his laptop,

putting it in front of me when he has found it. 'Sporting Opportunities Fund,' I say, reading the caption on a YouTube clip James wants me to see.

'You may find some of this familiar,' he says, as I watch this corporate dude from Australia making his pitch, which goes something like this: he will take your money and he will use it to bet on sporting events. Which, he says, might just be construed as gambling by some, but no more so than playing the stock market is gambling, or playing the property game is gambling – indeed, with the algorithmic sophistication that Sporting Opportunities Fund has in its armoury, the Australian suggests that this kind of sports betting is a more conservative option than the traditional markets in stocks and shares.

'He's good,' I say.

'I'm thinking of using this,' James says.

'Like, what I was doing was actually taking the conservative option?'

'Up to a point, yes.'

'The point being that this guy is actually telling people straight out he's going to back horses and dogs with their money, whereas I might have told them something else.'

'But you've admitted that.'

'Right.'

'We may use it for context . . . to show the culture . . . to get away from this idea that what you were running was a Ponzi scheme. In the accepted sense.'

'I was just ahead of my time,' I say, still marvelling at the shamelessness of the Australian.

But the Australian is also bringing back the anxiety. I can do without these visions of men having a wonderful time out there, doing more or less what I was doing but brazen enough to announce it, to put it on YouTube. I can do without images of betting as a profitable enterprise. I do not want to be reminded that gambling is only a problem if you lose.

Did the band play this hall in Castletown? Might have done. They played some hall out this way in which I recall that they blew all the electrics but I can't honestly say it was this one. It would seem too perfectly sad to be coming back here a lifetime later, not having made it to Carnegie Hall, just back to this same hall with nothing, absolutely nothing, except a desire to stop gambling.

James, empathising with all my discomforts, drives me out here. Castletown is not a village, just a crossroads with a few cottages joined together, a pub, a petrol station and the hall. We are here early, so we go to the pub. I offer to get a taxi home afterwards but James insists on waiting for me in the pub while I'm at the meeting, then driving me home.

We order a couple of pints of Guinness from the girl and sit in the lounge, near the fire. There is nobody else in the bar or the lounge, and still, given all the alternatives, I wouldn't mind staying here for a long time, drinking and thinking and undisturbed by the bullshit of this world.

Without intending or even wanting to do it, sedated perhaps by the quietness of this place and by the Guinness, I start to talk to James about Annie. Soon I am telling him everything about her. About how strange it has been since Ed first mentioned her name to be visited by these memories of her, to be burdened by the thought of that stupid twist of fate, to be wondering if any of it matters anymore. I tell him about the music in Ed's car setting me off the other night, as if James is my counsellor who will understand such things.

But he does not offer me an interpretation: he just accepts what I am saying and then he suggests a solution that is beautiful in its optimism, in its simplicity.

'Have you considered writing a letter to her?' he says.

'Never crossed my mind.'

'Maybe when this is over . . .'

'Ed thinks she's in Canada.'

'She liked you writing letters to her,' he says.

'Plenty of time for writing letters in jail,' I say.

'She might even write back,' he says, and I note that he declines to contradict me about being in jail, that he is still not offering me any illusions in this regard.

I raise my pint glass to him. 'I might even go to Canada,' I say.

I am thrilled by this notion that has just come to me, elated by it. Maybe it is the addict in me, always looking to be elated about something, but it is not the madness of it that appeals, it is the logic, how sensible and even obvious it seems. If I get away with this, I am going to have to live somewhere, and it's probably better all round if that place is far away from here . . . Canada, maybe Vancouver . . .

James neither encourages nor discourages me on this one, just nodding to acknowledge that it has registered with him. As we sit there sipping our Guinness, I am thinking about him, about how he seems to have avoided the traps that Ed and I walked into so happily, how he struck a much better deal with the gods, maybe handing over a little wildness, and getting in return such a fine temperament, a decent character.

Maybe he got the best break going too, not having Ed as a presence in his life, having instead the comradeship of Al-Anon, the encouragement. I wish that I had had such misfortune, that I had found myself the son of a degenerate, that I had received the sort of help that I am only getting now, when it is probably too late.

Tommy ran a post office in a large provincial town. He was married with a small daughter; the marriage was not going well. He started getting into a bit of trouble with the online betting, the more so because there was so much money coming into the post office, money that he was in charge of, at the end of every day.

In a period of about eighteen months he managed to lose about one and a half million of the post office's money, betting online on sports. He was a valued guest of a betting corporation at the Curragh and the Aviva stadium, people who must have known that a man running a post office could not be having bets of forty grand a time without access to dubious revenue streams. But they took the money anyway.

When there was an audit, he just changed the numbers by adding a digit, so that 58 grand might become 358 grand. Due to the incompetence and the negligence and the basic laziness of those who ran the institution, for a while it worked.

He hid it from everyone around him, too, somehow, though he would sometimes need to go to the toilet to vomit when a last-minute goal broke his heart. He remembers John Arne Riise's late own-goal in the Champions League semi-final between Liverpool and Chelsea as a terrible sickener, but there were plenty more like that.

He figures it can probably be traced back to his first bet, an accumulator on the first day at Cheltenham, which won him a couple of grand and gave him a feeling of such elation he spent the rest of his life trying to get it back.

When the post office finally worked out what was going on, Tommy went on the run. He drove up North, staying in a different hotel every night. He was missing for eleven days. His family were sure he had killed himself. But he was still alive and still gambling, even managing to have a bet of twenty grand on a horse in the Saturday racing, which won at odds of 4–6, his last winner, his last bet. That trip to the betting office helped to locate him, and now the hounds were coming to get him.

Tommy is with us in the lounge now, after the meeting. He is about thirty-five years old, a stocky sort of a chap wearing a hooded sweatshirt, with little in his demeanour that would tell you he once had forty grand on a football match in Iran on a Monday morning just because it was on. There is one thing: he talks very fast. You could imagine him rattling out the right answers to whatever questions the post office investigators might have had, but that only occurs to you because you know his story. He told it tonight from the chair, but he is able to tell it again for James. Like all the others I have heard in recent days, telling their stories, he doesn't mind that he will be telling it again and again in the years to come, because if he stops telling it, he fears he may forget some part of it, and with that he will forget the fear, and the sickness, and the madness.

He got three years, one suspended. Which is not encouraging for me.

But that was five years ago, when it wasn't officially a disease.

He pleaded guilty, too, but he wasn't surprised by the sentence. The part that killed him was that the guard put the handcuffs on him as he was being led to the van and a picture of him with the cuffs on appeared in the papers.

Sitting with him and the four other men who were at the meeting, I wish I wasn't hearing some of this. I wish I did not have that image in my head of the handcuffs, and now I do. But I've been getting something else from him too, from all

255

of them, that same air of lightness and of generosity that I got from the crowd at my first meeting, a sense that giving up this thing is really worth it, that it can give you a kind of second life. And we gamblers love that. We hate to think it's all over.

Tommy calls my chances of walking out of there at about 60–40. He doesn't say which is the sixty and which is the forty, and I don't ask him to clarify.

James is driving me home, uplifted by all that he has heard and by the company of men who are trying to make something of themselves. I calculate that he must have had at least four pints of Guinness, which means he is officially drink-driving again, apparently indifferent to the law and to the social stigma attached to this practice.

I would raise it with him, except I find it oddly endearing that he possesses this one really obvious character defect. It's as though he is so secure in his drinking and in his ability to handle it, that he doesn't even notice it. Or it could be an inheritance from his father that will cause him grief some day, maybe a load of grief.

'Tommy's story . . . amazing,' he says, as we boot along the country roads.

'Three years,' I say.

'The thing that really amazed me was that he didn't jump off a cliff or something when he was on the run. How could he face coming home to all that?'

'Well, if he'd killed himself, he couldn't have had that bet of twenty grand on the Saturday, right?'

'Right.'

'You don't think a man like that is going to kill himself with twenty grand still left in the tank, do you?'

We arrive back at the mobile home. James is still trying to figure out why Tommy didn't kill himself. 'OK, he had twenty grand to bet with but still he had time after the bet, with the police down in the lobby, to jump out the window of the hotel or something,' he says.

I light another cigarette, considering what he has said, and how normal people in general do not understand these matters.

'But the horse won,' I say.

CHAPTER 20

Ed rings me at three thirty-five in the morning.

I answer the call straight away, so he probably knows he didn't wake me up. But another person might have asked.

'Johnny, come down here and join us,' he says, maybe a little drunk.

'Got this court case tomorrow,' I say.

'So you're sitting up there not sleeping. How is that any good?'

'It's the best I can do, Ed.'

'If I don't see you tomorrow, I'll be thinking about you.'

'Thanks.'

'I've been thinking a lot about you these last few days.'

'Right . . . I'm sorry I lost your two grand.'

'Forget it.'

'And . . . sorry I lost the twenty-five grand after winning it.'

'Twenty-six grand, nearly twenty-seven . . .'

'I told you I couldn't do it . . . '

'Right again, Johnny . . . right again . . . '

There is a silence on the line, maybe half a minute, as if Ed has been distracted by one of his companions. Then: 'I'm thinking that your way may be the best way.'

'My way?'

'You and James . . . you know, giving it all up . . . going straight.'

'You're thinking that now?'

'I'm coming around to it.'

'Good for you.'

'No, Johnny, I didn't say it's for me.'

'Ah, right.'

'For you . . . for you, maybe.'

You don't need sleep when you are standing trial the next day. This I have found to be true.

You know that you will not be nodding off in the dock: you've got enough electricity running through you to keep you alert. And in my case I don't really want to sleep. I want to be fully conscious all night, because this may be my last night out here.

Should I have gone down to Ed's and drunk with him and whoever else was there with him, all those interesting people who can't get a drink anywhere else?

You don't need sleep when you are standing trial the next day, but you do need not to be drunk. This is my conclusion.

I am appreciating the solitude here, in this walk-through coffin of mine, after this day of meeting and talking and preparing, of that crowded coffee shop where all those people who don't know me decide they know me anyway. I am enjoying this solitude.

The night goes on for a very long time when you are awake, maybe even long enough to write a letter to some girl you loved when you were sixteen. But not this night, I think, and not when there is no proper writing paper or maybe a Parker pen – dear God, from out of the great emptiness I remember that I used to write those things with a Parker pen.

But I also want to keep the thought of that letter alive until after the verdict tomorrow. Just the prospect of it may get me through some badness, if badness awaits me – if my relocation to, say, Vancouver needs to be put back for, say, three years, or four years, or seven years.

Ah, yes, one thing I am finding is that the crazy dreams of a desperate man do not seem to him that crazy at all.

I have all three bars of the Super Ser on, though tonight is not as cold as the nights just gone. I have not bothered to throw away all the broken bits of the laptop – I like the idea that they will probably still be there when I come back , whenever that is. I like the fact that I am still scrunching my cigarette butts into the floor, without even thinking about it.

Solitude in the middle of the night is a thing to cherish, when in a few hours you will be getting out of a taxi and the press photographers and the reporters and the TV cameras will be there, looking for a piece of you. I always believed there was some deep wisdom in the primitive idea that the photographer steals some of your soul when he takes your picture, and it is worse in my case because I have already traded so much of my soul, or just surrendered it.

I have a little piece of it left, though, and I am hanging on to that. I was protecting it when I smashed the machine that is lying there all busted; I was fighting for it.

They don't know I still have it, those people who will be creeping all over me tomorrow, but I will know it.

My taxi driver is here at nine thirty, ten minutes early, the same one as yesterday, Tony the Serb or the Romanian or the Bulgarian. I don't want to know where he is from: I want us to keep that mystery between us. And I guess he wants to be on time for a man who will throw him a fifty-euro note for the trip.

I give him a little salute as I get into the back seat, and he salutes me back, correctly sensing that I am saluting him because I can't bring myself to say anything, even hello. That any talking on this journey will come from me, not from him. I am shutting down now. I will protect what I have. I will not allow myself any sentimental feelings on this journey.

I had a blast of feelings just before I left the caravan, opening the wardrobe and looking at what is left of my fine clothes, picking out my one sober suit for this show, the one I had for funerals. And then I opened that race card one last time, the one from the Phoenix Park, and I went through all the pages, and I thought about my father, and how he would give me back the money I had lost. How he said the words that started my life as a card player: 'Let's make this a bit more interesting.' He married the wrong woman. I made a few unfortunate choices too.

But enough. I am being driven through the village and into the town but I am freezing it all out. Even Ed's house stirs up nothing for me. It's as if I have this cool room inside me, containing the one thing that will get me through this day: the certain knowledge that I am not who they think I am. They think I am a gambler. I know that I am a gambler who is getting out of the game, at least for today. The difference between these two states of being is infinite.

'The guy who runs that place is an old friend of mine,' I say, as we pass Ed's.

'He owns the taxi,' Tony says, and he laughs.

'Ah, he never mentioned that,' I say.

'Owns a lot of things,' Tony says.

'Terrible place,' I say, gesturing back towards the house.

'Not as bad as you'd think,' Tony says.

I see that James is waiting for me outside the courthouse,

watching out for the cab. I see also that the journalists and photographers are there, but they haven't seen me yet.

James walks towards the cab, trying to seem nonchalant. But the press have figured it out, and they are coming to meet me too.

I reach into my pocket and peel off a fifty for Tony. I get a better thought, and decide to give him two fifties. And then I get the best thought. I give him the whole bundle, the guts of a grand.

I might have done a few people out of a few million, but I was never mean.

James leads me up the steps of the great courthouse, while the journalists and photographers do their job. I take note of the television camera to my right, and I try to set my demeanour, to visualise what I will look like on the main evening news, walking up these steps.

The barrister is waiting inside, in his robes. James introduces him to me, this Maurice Field, who seems just slightly older than James but probably went to a better school, given his accent and the sense of vigorous self-esteem he communicates with a handshake, how sincerely pleased he sounds to be representing me, and to be himself.

He is one of several barristers in the hall, several solicitors and gardaí and many others with some interest in the proceedings, with cases of their own to win or to lose, all of it conveying such a powerful sense of man's corruption that in their company I am inclined to see myself as a reasonably straightforward human being.

If I had the choice, if you had lined up all these barristers against the wall and asked me to choose, I might well have gone for Maurice Field, compared to some of the older advocates in the room, the ones who have perhaps spent too many years enriching themselves on the delicacies of human destruction, who make my guy look like an idealist of some sort, maybe even a Romantic poet.

In a group I see Thomas Gaskin and his people, who seem to be pretending that I am not in the hall but otherwise look like well-off country people who are on the whole satisfied with life. I guess they will always find a few quid if they're looking for it. They're expecting the right result today, a day they have probably been looking forward to for a long time. In their place I, too, would be giving off an air of satisfaction; I would be seeing this as the end of a hard road. They have come here to see me go down, and I do not resent them for that. I did them a terrible wrong.

They don't know me either, no more than any of these people know me, know this change in me.

I am so fucked with tension now, wired by this atmosphere of completely respectable sleaze, that I have a desperate desire to ask James if I should go outside again to smoke a cigarette. But I know I can't because I don't want them to see that on the six o'clock news.

You would think that after about half a million gambles, all those surrenderings to the power of another, I would have a way of getting through these moments, a method, a system that would shut down all the normal responses, kill the fear, anaesthetise all emotions. But I am just like anyone else right now: a frightened man at the mercy of the forces of the universe.

I am trying to join the small talk of my two lawmen, but I am not even hearing it anymore. I have seen a man sweeping through the crowd to the door of the courtroom, where he stands waiting as if he wants to get the best seat. It is Ed Brennan, looking as fresh as Ed Brennan will ever look, after another night's drinking. Looking so fresh, and keen, and strong, he seems to draw much of the energy of the people in this hall to his presence, some of them looking, some of them pretending not to look.

I do not think it through but I have no need to think it through because, seeing him there, I have the strongest hunch I think I have ever had in a long, long career in the hunch business. I think we are going to win this thing.

CHAPTER 21

Tony the taximan must have felt it too, in his bones. Coming down the steps with Ed on one side and James on the other, with a three-year suspended sentence against my name, and a lot of conditions attached that I can handle, I see Tony waiting there and he sees me. He raises his fist as if he, too, has been liberated.

We do not stop to answer any questions from the media, we do not even discuss our own arrangements, we just know that we are getting into that taxi together, that we are bound by a superior force, by the elation of the day.

I get into the back of the car with Ed, leaving the passenger seat to James. With the photographers snapping at us, Ed calls out to the driver to take him to his place. And since nobody has any other suggestions to make, it looks like we're going back to Ed's, for the first time in a long time.

We are all a bit delirious, too high right now to be talking about how it happened – and, anyway, I think I know how it happened.

I think the judge's name was on that list, that he saw Ed in court and that he knew what he had to do. I think he seemed distracted and he seemed confused and he seemed unhappy. But I also think that James put the case together strongly enough to allow the judge to make that decision without being impeached. To make a statement about addiction that would sound reasonable and even progressive. To go in hard on the bookmakers, who encouraged my addiction by entertaining me in their corporate boxes.

That's what I think, but I could be wrong.

Right now, driving away from the courthouse instead of being led into a van wearing handcuffs, I do not care what is right or what is wrong.

We are at the far side of the town, about to turn to take the coast road out to the village, when James indicates that he wants Tony to stop the car. He turns to face Ed. 'The judge . . . he's on the list, isn't he?' he says.

It's the first time I have heard James talking to Ed, and I can sense that he is guarded, that Ed was right: they don't really know one another.

Ed strikes a calm attitude, shaking his head as if shocked that such a weird thought might intrude. 'Fuck, no,' he says.

'No?'

'Really . . . no.'

James looks ahead with an expression of amusement. Then he turns back to Ed. 'So, you know all the names?' he says.

'And a few who aren't even written down,' Ed says.

James is not satisfied. 'I suppose when you say the judge is not on the list, you might mean that he's not on it anymore.'

'I mean he was never on it,' Ed says.

James looks at Tony, as if the driver might give away some clue. Then he turns to Ed, sitting there looking innocent. Then he starts to laugh. 'So, you didn't get the vibe in there?' he says.

Ed shifts himself forward in the seat. 'The vibe I got was that you guys won.'

'The judge's body language?'

'Body language, my hole.'

James backs off, thinking about it. He smiles as if he is enjoying the repartee. Then he turns back to face Ed. 'I don't believe you,' he says. Now he is organising himself to get out of the car, checking something in his briefcase. I don't want him to go like this, without celebration.

'You are the man, James, you are the main man,' I say. I reach out and shake his hand.

He takes a book out of his briefcase, Dostoyevsky's *The Gambler*. 'I got this for you, win or lose,' he says.

268

'Thank you.' I open the paperback, enjoying the smell of the pages, the texture of the paper, all those words honestly written that tell me I am returning to civilisation. I stopped reading good books about twenty years ago.

'Johnny's read all the books,' Ed says.

'We'll have a few drinks, come on,' I say to James, envisaging some marvellous scene of reconciliation after many drinks and smokes, out at the house.

James sits there, assessing the situation. This would be the first time he has been asked to Ed's place, by anyone. He is perhaps not ready for it.

'Come on, James,' I say.

'Another time, yes,' he says. And I think he means it – he means most things he says.

'Tomorrow?' Ed says, with a kind of understatement, like they're in and out of each other's places all the time.

James gets out of the car and shuts the door. He asks for the window to be wound down. He doesn't say yes to Ed's invitation; he doesn't say no. 'Four men in a car . . . never looks right,' he says.

As he starts to walk back to the town, I feel compelled to go after him, to ask him one more time to come out to the house today and not tomorrow, to reassure him that he really did win this case, or that it couldn't have been won without his wisdom and generosity, that nothing should take that away from him. I think he would really like me to do that. But I also feel compelled not to go after him, because in my mind I am already in another place.

Ed gives Tony a tap on the shoulder and we are on our way to that place.

Tony wants to talk to me. Ed is striding towards his front door, but Tony keeps me sitting in the back seat, insisting that I take back the money I gave him. He thinks I will need it now.

Still juiced up with the good adrenalin, I make a sound and fair decision to accept half the money, and then, like gentlemen, we go inside.

It is true what Tony said: the place is not as bad as you'd think. Ed leads me briskly through the hall and into the lounge, which is a lounge in every sense, a large room in a house designed in the early 1970s, and a lounge bar with couches and tables with ashtrays on them. I knew this room well, I am remembering it and yet I am trying not to remember it too clearly.

I hand my coat to Ed, like some aristocrat about to play the tables. He takes it to a hanger beside the bar, on which the coats of so many down-going men have been placed.

The drinks are dispensed at a small counter in the corner, with a few optics for whiskey or vodka, and Guinness and Heineken on tap. And at the other end of the room is the fireplace, which throws me into a flashback, with its overdone brickwork, the way it draws attention to itself, the fact that it has a little seating area built into the front of it. I sat there, many times.

And there are the many burns on the carpet and the stench

of stale smoke, so unfamiliar now in any drinking room in this country, any room at all. It is not just last night's smoke, it is the last one thousand nights' smoke, consolidated.

Ed takes a Dyson vacuum cleaner from behind the counter and gives the carpet a quick blast with it. He empties a few ashtrays. I am reminded of his family inheritance, his skill as a barman, his ease of movement in those tight spaces.

I start to laugh at this burst of efficiency, the way that the slob who's been hanging out in my caravan is suddenly transformed when he returns to his own drinking place. He closes the curtains, which run the whole length of the room.

'We're closed tonight,' he says.

'I was hoping to meet some of the great old characters who come here.'

Tony is doing some chores behind the bar. It seems that he is more to Ed than just a taxi driver, but I do not have the energy to enquire.

I throw myself back on a couch. That adrenalin, that juice is flooding out of me. I think it is flooding out of Ed, too. It's like a great weariness has come into the lounge to join us. Or maybe it is not weariness, but peace.

Ed settles into a couch opposite me, rubbing his temples as if to release some solution from his brain. I think I recognise that couch, which is at once both reassuring and unbearably disturbing.

Tony places the drinks in front of us. Mine looks good, gin with ice and lime. It tastes good, a gimlet as they used to call a gin'n'lime in the gangster movies.

Ed raises his glass to me, a salute.

'You fixed the judge, right?' I say.

'No,' he says.

'You had him fixed all along.'

'No,' he says.

'He looked nervous to me . . . James picked it up too.'

He eases himself up from the couch and over to the bar, to add more gin to his drink. 'There are a lot of reasons in this world for a man to be nervous,' he says.

On the long table in front of me there is a pack of cards. They are well-used, decorated with kitsch images of Ireland. I take them out and start to shuffle them.

Ed brings his drink back to the table. He also brings the bottle of gin.

I remember his call to me at three thirty-five in the morning. 'You admit that you were wrong so? That James's way was better than yours?' I say.

'That would appear to be the case,' he says.

Magnanimous as he is being here, still I find it hard to believe him, about anything. And I know him. For those who don't know him at all, or who know him only by reputation, you can understand why his presence in that courtroom, supporting a particular side, might lead to a certain excitement.

If he had fixed it from the start, I ask myself, would he not have just told me about it? No, I don't think that would be his way, and then again, maybe he fixed it, but not from the start. Or maybe my first instinct was right, that he fixed it but the contribution of James was also important in giving the judge a kind of alibi, the most plausible combination in a land in which even the best are at least half-corrupted.

A lot of gin and lime is going down, and every time I try to get a clear picture of Ed's precise relationship to all the parties in this case, I find him slipping away into the mist of possibilities because that is where he lives.

And one of these possibilities is that he did nothing at all, except offer his moral and financial support to his old friend, in the most good-hearted fashion, which I can believe too. For a while. And that he was helping his son, like any father would, without wanting any credit for it.

But, yes, a lot of gin and lime is going down, and it is feeling beautiful to be here drinking it, instead of eating some gruel for supper in a midlands prison.

This lounge is not a happy place for any good-living person, but it is just about perfect for the other kind. I am remembering nights here, when we used to sit up late, plotting our journey to a place we never got to, never got near. There were musical instruments all over this carpet sometimes, and amplifiers, and people.

What there is now is a long wall with many shelves full of vinyl records, thousands of them. And on a ledge below one of the shelves there is the fabulous stereo, the same one with the big speakers out of which Led Zeppelin would come roaring, and Derek and the Dominos, with Ed playing the drums, playing them so hard, and with such authority, it seemed certain he would make a life out of it. But he never got to that.

The two of us sit there, silent for a while.

'Does it work?' I say, gesturing to the stereo.

'It sure does.'

'You listen to all the old songs?'

'I sit here on this couch, and I drink, and I listen. Sometimes I have a good cry,' he says.

'You still have some stuff up there,' I say, gazing at the albums, so many treasures.

'What could be any better than this, Johnny?'

He is looking straight at me now, and in his voice there is a note of sincerity. I start to examine the records more closely, first by looking at the titles on the spines, many of them crazily familiar to my eye, then by flicking through them.

'Canada . . . I'm thinking of going to Canada,' I say, as I recognise the albums one after another, as each one fills my soul with longing for the future I was going to have.

'Pick one record,' he says, as if laying down a challenge. He has just declined to comment on what I said about going to Canada, as James did, but perhaps not for the same reason. James, I felt, didn't want me making plans in case I was disappointed, and it was actually James who suggested that I write a letter, whereas Ed probably regards this talk of Canada as so eccentric as to be undeserving of comment. I let it go. I don't fancy making that case at the end of this day.

He wants me to pick one but I can't pick one album by going through them and making a selection because I fear the psychic trauma to which it might lead. I can only close my eyes and pick one. I pick *Darkness On the Edge of Town*.

There is Springsteen, standing against the venetian blinds in his white T-shirt and black jacket, a picture I must have stared at for a long time, as I tended to do when I was listening to albums. There is the title of the album and the name of the artist rattled out on an old typewriter. Maybe it's the unfamiliar largeness of the twelve-inch sleeve, but I am getting a slightly different perspective on that picture now. I see that Bruce was trying to convey an overall idea of him being a blue-collar guy living in this kinda run-down place, with the blinds and cheap wallpaper, whereas originally I saw Bruce essentially as a rock star acting out the part of the blue-collar guy, signalling that this was where he was coming from.

I guess that the original perception was the right one, that as I have grown older I have, if anything, become more accepting of illusion, somehow more naive.

'I've gone off Bruce,' I say.

'No, you haven't,' he says.

I take out the inner sleeve, with the lyrics all laid out there, to be stared at when you had finished staring at the outer sleeve. I have a shiver of recognition as it strikes me that I first heard the voice of Springsteen in this room, on this record player, on this album. That my first thought was how like Elvis he sounded, singing 'Badlands'.

'Back where we started,' I say.

He laughs, his original laugh. 'It's great, isn't it?' he says.

He takes the Springsteen album from me and replaces the inner sleeve with the briskness of a man who is still tidy about his albums. He puts it back in the exact place it was taken from, another reflex. He moves deliberately to another section, and as he picks out an album almost without hesitation, I realise they are still organised in alphabetical order. He takes out *Veedon Fleece*: he is going to play 'Linden Arden Stole The Highlights', not on the little YouTube speaker but in full stereophonic sound, a thing I have not heard since everything ended for me.

I look at the sleeve of the album, with Van and the Irish Wolfhounds on the grass and I can see it there beside that turntable at two in the morning such a long time ago, with Ed pouring the vodka and the white lemonade.

This record was made a few years before our time; we came to it late, but we got there. And by the look of us today, we probably never got beyond there; we couldn't even imagine that there was any other place to go after this.

From the sleeve he takes a twelve-inch vinyl disc, a thing I have not seen for a long time, an antique belonging to some era of limitless indulgence. He takes the record to the turntable, the oversized model that still looks luxuriously big and powerful. He lifts the lid delicately and switches on the machine. The turntable spins. There is a softness that has settled on him in this room, a sense that there is some mysterious presence in here that he does not want to disturb. He examines the disc, selecting the right track, showing some skill in the handling to keep from smudging it with his fingerprints. He puts the record on the turntable.

'I'm just trying to figure out how many nights we spent in here,' I say.

'Very many,' he says.

I am inclined to envy him, and whatever he has found in this place, in this long-gone time. Like his determination to drink himself to death without complaint or remorse, there is something pure about it. He holds the needle over the album to drop it on track two, side one, as I recall.

But I can't take it. I can't listen to these sounds anymore. I have had enough of these indestructible memories. I do not want to be mad with melancholia anymore, mad as I was that night on the promenade when I could hear the music coming out of the amusements again, the music of my youth. I do not care that in this room I sat with Annie and she gave me the signal and I missed it. I do not care about that because I was just a boy, that's all, I was just a boy. I can even see the place against the wall where we were sitting that night, but it brings me no more grief: it is nothing to me anymore, it is nothing, because tonight, I feel that all the things that have gone wrong in my life can be put right again. That I am fucking blessed.

I lift the needle before the song starts, that piano. I take the record off the deck and hand it to Ed, who just shrugs. He puts it back into the sleeve and replaces it on the shelf. Taking his mood from me, it seems. There is no sense of him having a sentimental attachment anymore: he is acting like a guy who works in a record shop, just arranging his stock.

Back at the table I take to shuffling the cards again, and I start to deal. Pontoon.

We play a few games, for no money, sticking and twisting and drinking.

Then a notion comes to me to play a different kind of game. I take that bundle of notes out of my pocket, that monkey, and I put it on the table. 'Let's make this a bit more interesting,' I say.

Ed sits back on the couch, picking at his lower lip. He looks at the money on the table and then he looks to Tony, as if some guidance might come from him, but Tony is just watching and drinking. 'I thought you had retired,' he says.

'I just got out of jail.'

'You're drunk?'

'Just happy.'

'I thought it was working for you . . . that bullshit . . .'

'Let it work tomorrow.'

'So, this is, like, your night off from it?' he says.

I raise my glass in agreement. 'It's what my father used to say . . . Let's make this a bit more interesting.'

I deal him two cards, and two for myself. I look at my cards, a king and a jack, an excellent hand for the dealer. I wait for him to pick up his cards, and to put his money down. Ed is sweating now, rubbing his temples, engaged with all the vital forces of his being, wanting so much to do the wrong thing, struggling so hard against what is right. He leans across the table. He fixes his eyes on mine and I stare back at him. He places his hand on the two cards in front of him and pushes them back towards me, and now I am starting to see him more clearly. Now he is coming out of the mist.

'I couldn't take your money,' he says.

I let out a half-drunk whoop of victory, and he starts to smile, realising that he fell for it.

'Good one, Johnny,' he says.

I take hold of the bottle of gin to pour him another drink, to make it up to him. He rattles his glass on the table, demanding that I fill it, and enough of my little games. He watches me pouring the gin until the glass is full.

I take the money off the table and put it back in my pocket.

'I'll need this anyway, if I'm going to Canada.'

Ed studies me with an air of resignation, as if there's nothing he can do to help me now. He throws the whole pack of cards at me.

'Let's make this a bit more interesting . . .' He is enjoying the phrase, mocking it.

Maybe it's interesting enough already, I am thinking.

Maybe it is interesting enough.

And what if he had put his bet down, and played me for the money?

Well, I just figured he wouldn't. It was an intuition on my part.

It was, if you like, a gamble.

ACKNOWLEDGEMENTS

I would like to thank Caroline and Katie and Roseanne and Adam for their love and encouragement, and my agent Faith O'Grady and publisher Ciara Considine for doing so much to get this done. My friends Dion Fanning, Brian Hendley, Paul Howard, Geoffrey Byrne, Paul Cleary and Noel Byrne were always there or thereabouts. And thanks to my late father Frank, who showed me how to bet responsibly.